A Gross
Carriage of
Justice

A Gross
Carriage of
Justice

Robert L. Fish

© Copyright 1979 by Robert L. Fish
First e-reads publication 1999
www.e-reads.com
ISBN 0-7592-0494-2

Other works by Robert L. Fish

also available in e-reads editions

The Murder League
The Shrunken Head

This book is affectionately dedicated to the memory
of
Alice-Mary Schnirring
The-Mouse-That-Roared

A Gross
Carriage of
Justice

1

When Clarence Wellington Alexander was a youngster in grade school back in his native village of Wapakeneta, Ohio, his home-room teacher told Mr. and Mrs. Alexander that their son would go far. What the teacher failed to add, out of consideration for the hard-working parents, was that she only wished Clarence would do it as soon as possible. For Clarence had been endowed, among other attributes, with a streak of larceny that would have done justice to a much older person — Caligula, possibly. In his formative years he had spent only as much time on his books as had been required; the rest of his efforts went toward developing what he himself recognized early could be cultivated into quite a lucrative talent.

It was not that Clarence did not have other talents. His ability at mimicry might have eventually led him into a career in show business, except that by the time Clarence had reached the eighth grade, he knew that not only was show business too slow a road to success, it was also honest, and there was something about honesty that rubbed Clarence the wrong way. He much preferred to use his ability to imitate voices to gather dirt from unsuspecting schoolmates on the telephone, and then use the information for blackmail. This, together with a few other dishonest ploys, enabled Clarence to live in a style not normally enjoyed by a twelve-year-old given ten cents a week allowance.

Growing maturity did not dim his wit, nor age wither his skill; nor, for that matter, did it improve his morals. By the time he had reached the eleventh grade his ability to imitate the voices of several teachers (male) in clandestine conversations with other teachers (female) added to his gross, so that when at last Clarence took his departure from Wapakeneta just prior to graduation, he left at night and driving a car which even his aging parents in their naïveté would scarcely have imagined had been gained from a newspaper route.

Of medium height and slender build, with heart-warming brown eyes and hair the color of burnt umber, and with a smile of innocence that would steal your heart or anything else lying about loose, Clarence marched through life. There were no absolutes in the philosophy of C. W. Alexander. In the manner of his namesake, in Clarence's grasp for the world anything was fair game, from the raffle fund for new high-school band uniforms which he had promoted just prior to his departure from his birthplace, to the gilt-edged securities which later were to provide many a widow with guaranteed pauperhood. To Clarence, if it moved it was game. William Shakespeare, stuck for a sharp bit of dialogue toward the end of *Julius Caesar*, has Brutus remark to Cassius, "There is a tide in the affairs of men which taken at the flood leads on to fortune." Clarence W. Alexander would have put it more succinctly: "When Opportunity knocks, open your ears!" One is forced to wonder just how far William Shakespeare might have gone had he possessed Clarence's command of the language.

All in all, Clarence had small reason to distrust his philosophy. By keeping his ears open to Opportunity's knock — and even at times leading Opportunity to his door with a twisted arm and helping it raise the knocker — Clarence had managed to reach the ripe age of thirty-seven without ever having suffered either hunger or the stigma of honest labor. True, there had been an occasional hiatus in his march upward and onward when some fractious judge had removed him from circulation for a time, but those occasions were rare. It was also true at times that Clarence had been forced to abandon his native strand for safer shores until certain memories weakened, and the time of which we speak was one of those. At the moment Clarence was residing in the old Avery farmhouse on the outskirts of the small village of Crumley-under-Chum in the shire of Sussex, in England.

The cause of this unfortunate exile still struck Clarence as being eminently unfair. It struck him that if some foreigner could sell a United States citizen the London Bridge with impunity — and in pieces, yet — that it was extremely inequitable to frown upon his simple reciprocity with the Golden Gate Bridge, especially since the Golden Gate was not only intact but earning money.

But frowned upon it had been, and so we find Clarence in England. He had chosen the small village of Crumley-under-Chum because he preferred small towns rather than large cities with large police forces. He also knew from his experience growing up in Wapakeneta, that the vaunted curiosity of the rural villager was grossly exaggerated. In general he knew the normal rural villager was far too busy trying to maintain his own privacy to spend much time worrying about violating the privacy of others.

His companion in exile was one Harold Nishbagel, a massive character in his early forties who was built along the lines of an earth-mover, with hands the size of football helmets, with spiky black hair, eyes like jaw-breakers, and a brow so low he looked as if he were perpetually peering under a picket fence. The two had met in prison, where Harold had managed to convince the most recalcitrant that there was nothing comical about the name "Harold," while the name "Nishbagel" had a positively royal ring to it. Since Clarence W. Alexander avoided violence as something he knew he was ill-equipped to cope with, and since Harold Nishbagel avoided thinking for much the same reason, the partnership seemed a natural one.

At the moment Clarence and Harold were seated on a bench running the length of the interior of the Deer's Head Pub on the main street of Crumley-under-Chum. Harold was carefully reading the Sunday supplement — in color — of a London journal he had found abandoned on the bench, his mug of ale forgotten beside him, his lips moving laboriously as his thick forefinger led him from word to word, much as a seeing-eye dog might lead a hesitant master over unfamiliar terrain. The newspaper was not current, but that was of small moment to Harold; on those rare occasions when he read, he did so strictly for entertainment.

At his side, Clarence stared balefully at the stuffed deer's head on one wall which had undoubtedly led some inspired publican in the past to the brilliant selection of the pub's name. The deer, in Clarence's considered opinion, had not died from shaft or shell, but most probably from drinking the premises' beer. There was a murmur from Harold as the gist of the story he was perusing finally worked its way through the intervening bone and reached the gray cells. He shook his head in sympathetic admiration.

"Chee!" he said in his gravel voice. "Ain't that nice!"

He nodded his Cro-Magnon-type head a few times in confirmation of his conclusion, and went back to deciphering the rest of the story. It would have been easier, he felt, if the British knew how to spell, but even with this added handicap he was proud to know he had overcome the worst of the communication problem and had the general sense of the article pretty well pinned to the mat.

Clarence looked over at Harold, a frown on his face. It was not that his consideration of the stuffed deer's head — which seemed to be considering him in return with equal or superior distaste — had led to any conclusions that were very profound, or even potentially profitable. It was simply that Clarence disliked having his thoughts disrupted, particularly by a flannel-brain like Harold. He glared at his companion.

"What?"

"It's these three old guys, see?" Harold said, his normally rough voice softening as memory of what he had just struggled through came back to him. "They got their picture here in the paper, see? In color."

He pointed; Clarence yawned. Harold went back to his story, his sausage-like finger keeping pace obediently.

"They was old friends, see, real old friends from way back, like. Then one of them gets in this jam, see, and the other two guys — they ain't got much money, you understand, in fact they're broke, see — but anyways, they hock their shirt, see, and go out and hire this big-shot mouthpiece he costs a fortune, but the old guys they don't care, and the mouthpiece, he springs the guy, see, but it leaves the three old guys broker than a '26 Model T and then what do you think happens?"

"They all go play potsie," Clarence said, and yawned again.

"Naw," Harold said a trifle disdainfully. It was not often that he held the advantage over Clarence where facts were concerned. "Naw. Instead they get a wad of dough from some funny-named bunch, some foundation, whatever that is. For bein' so self-sacrificin', see?" He looked up, his eyes shining, glistening with emotion. "Tell the truth, Clare, ain't that nice?"

Clarence was about to snort in derision when he suddenly felt that old familiar tingle. Was Opportunity attempting to rap on his door again, and was he trying to stuff his ears with cotton-wool? He put down his mug of beer — not with regret — and held out his hand demandingly.

"Let me see the paper."

There was a note of finality in the smaller man's voice that Harold recognized. He sighed in defeat and held the newspaper out, clutching it for one last instant to extract a condition.

"Read it out loud to me, huh, Clare? Huh?"

"Okay, okay." Clarence took the paper, folded it lengthwise in subway fashion to eliminate the possible intrusion of any truss ads, studied the pictures of the three old men a moment, shuddering a bit at the color of the fat one's garment — for Clarence was a bit of a Beau Brummel himself — and then began.

> "Gibraltah, Septembah 12:
> "The winnahs of lest yeah's Jahvis — "

4

Harold giggled. "No, do it straight, Clare."

"It's a British newspaper, so I thought you wanted it authentic," Clarence said. He was feeling better. Even the slight possibility of old man Opportunity's being in the neighborhood had that effect on him, and he had a strong hunch that at most old Opportunity wasn't any farther away than a few doors down the street. "Well, all right, if you insist. You're from Chicago, originally, aren't you? Well, get ready — here it is in pure Cicero."

"Aw, no," Harold said, serious now. "Just read it straight, please, huh, Clare?"

Clarence sighed. "You certainly make it difficult," he said, "but all right. Here it is:

> "Gibraltar, September 12:
> The winners of last year's Jarvis

Greater-Love-Hath-No-Man Foundation award for selfless consideration of one's fellow man, named for Harley P. Jarvis, whose life was
saved when a native bearer sprang between him and a charging rogue
elephant just moments after Jarvis had been forced to whip the fellow,
are at present enjoying the warm sunshine of Gibraltar after a pleasant
cruise on the luxurious steamer S.S. *Sunderland*, and are planning upon
returning to England on Friday next by way of Air Gibraltar."

Clarence paused, frowning.

"Friday next," he said half to himself, and checked the date line of the story again. He glanced at his wrist watch for the current date. "Hey! That's tomorrow." He thought for several more moments, and then continued.

"Readers of this journal are undoubtedly familiar with the piteous
but heart-warming story of the three old men, devoted friends and the
founders of the prestigious Mystery Authors Club of Great Britain, but
for those who purchase the *Times* or other lesser journals, we are pleased
to repeat the touching history.

"Last year, one of the steadfast trio, Clifford Simpson (at the left in
the accompanying photograph) was falsely accused of murder and
might well have been unjustly — but just as thoroughly — hanged had
it not been for his two friends, William Carruthers and Timothy Briggs
(center and right respectively in the accompanying photograph). Not
once did their faith in their friend's innocence waver! Not once did
they allow the overwhelming circumstantial evidence or their own
extreme poverty to distract them from the vital task of seeing to their
friend's release from his gyves.

5

"(He wasn't actually gyved, of course — Ed.)

"Although poor as church mice, the two old men sold their meager possessions, and by means which, out of pride, they refuse to reveal to this day, they managed to employ the famous barrister. Sir Percival Pugh. Sir Percival, although known to be adamant in demanding and receiving extremely high fees, somehow was paid — at what sacrifice by the three friends we may never know. But having extracted his pound of flesh. Sir Percival, with his admitted genius, proved to one and all that Mr. Simpson had been the innocent victim of circumstance, and deserved praise rather than censure for his role in the unfortunate affair.

"As a result of the self-sacrifice of the friends, each for the other, they were jointly awarded last year's laurels from the Jarvis Greater-Love-Hath-No-Man Foundation and with the huge sum which accompanies this prestigious award, the three old friends — old both in years as well as in the uplifting experience nurtured over more than five decades — are spending a few days in Gibraltar after enjoying a pleasant cruise on the S.S. *Sunderland*.

"We can only raise our editorial hats and say: Gentlemen, welcome back! Friday next we shall be pleased to have you once again on British soil! England is proud of you!"

Clarence put the newspaper down and frowned off into space for several moments, after which his frown turned into a pleasant though thoughtful smile. His mind, accustomed to producing intricate plans at short notice, was already busily working on the present problem, and he had no doubt it would come up with something appropriate at the proper time, if not before. Harold, watching his friend for comment, misinterpreted the smile.

"Nice, huh, Clare? Them old guys stickin' together like that?"

"Yes," Clarence said, and went on planning.

"Like that time in Quentin, we had these two guys, always fightin', and then one day — "

Clarence looked at him.

"I said, yes," he said in a tone that ended the discussion. At the moment there was no time for thoughts to be disrupted. It was, though, as Harold had said, very nice, indeed. Three old men with more money than they needed for their obviously limited years . . . . It was not that Clarence lacked sufficient funds at the moment; actually, his Arab customer had paid the first two installments on the sale of the Golden Gate Bridge before he became suspicious when he saw that police cars were not required to pay at the toll booth; he was sure that was not what free enterprise was all about. No, it was not that Clarence lacked money. It was simply that he felt there was no sense in giving old man Opportunity a free ride, in letting old O sit around with his hands in his pockets when there was money to be made. One never knew when a little extra cash might come in handily. Besides, there were just so many bridges in the world, and there was no guarantee that oil would come out of the ground forever.

Admittedly, time was short if the three old men were returning on the morrow, but this of itself did not bother Clarence. He was sure he would come up with some scheme in the required time. Of course, the scenario would have to be adaptable to the cast of characters. One had to recognize, for example, that the promise of exorbitant profits sometime in the distant future for some non-existent oil well soon to be drilled would scarcely hold much lure for men of an advanced age. And asking them to invest in a pornographic movie studio in order to meet nubile young actresses was probably equally pointless. Nor even getting them in some crap game in an alley using his educated dice; at their age they undoubtedly had trouble sitting, let alone squatting or kneeling.

Clarence studied the benign and fleshy features of the corpulent man in the bilious mustard-colored suit, and smiled to himself. It would be a bit like clubbing carp in a rain barrel, he admitted to himself, but if he couldn't sell a fake-genuine diamond stickpin, or a gold brick, to anyone with that taste in clothes, he would retire and take up needlepoint. No, he decided, the best way was the easiest way. Just take the money away from them as quickly and painlessly as possible, send them about their business, and go on about life.

His mind made up and the little wheels in his head now purring along beautifully, meshing with lovely synchronization as he perfected the final details of his basically simple plan, Clarence came to his feet and tilted his head toward the bar.

"Order something while I check on Gibraltar Air schedules, will you, Hal?" he asked. "Something," he added, thinking about it, "other than beer."

"Air schedules?" Harold asked, confused. "Hey, Clare, why do you want air schedules? We can't go home yet, can we? We goin' someplace different, Clare?"

But Harold was addressing a vacant bench, for Clarence was already at the telephone booth, leafing through the proper volume for the number of Air Gibraltar. It was a pity that Clarence did not have the prescience to pay a visit on Sir Percival Pugh, or even to chat with Captain Manley-Norville of the S.S. *Sunderland*, asking for all available information regarding the three old men. In that case there is no doubt that Clarence would have dropped the telephone book like a hot offer of respectable employment and would have returned, with gratitude, to his drink, whatever it was, shaking his head at his narrow escape . . . .

7

2

As a result of one of those very odd coincidences which are the despair of statisticians but the delight of authors needing them for their plots, the very same edition of the very same Sunday supplement in color which had intrigued Clarence Alexander with its financial possibilities — and which had so warmed the cockles of Harold Nishbagel's heart — on the very next morning was having quite an opposite effect upon one of the three subjects of the article. Timothy Briggs, seated with Clifford Simpson at a small metal table on the veranda of their modest hotel in Gibraltar, put aside his brandy, took no notice of the champagne nestling in a bucket at his side, and gripped his copy of the Sunday supplement crushingly as he read the article for a second time. He shook his head and sneered openly.

" . . . after *enjoying* a *pleasant* cruise on the *luxurious* S.S. *Sunderland!*" he quoted with blistering sarcasm. "That miserable tub!"

Timothy Briggs was a tiny mite of a man with a temper that easily made up for his lack of size. His iron-gray hair seemed to stand on end, as if from the electricity generated by his own jerky but constant movements, or by his explosive temperament; it made him look like an upright bath brush suffering from static. His small face, seamed with a network of wrinkles, was dominated by his small but exceedingly sharp, snapping black eyes. Timothy Briggs, it often seemed to his two friends, went through life demanding to be taken advantage of, just so he could properly respond. Nor — at least to his own mind — was he often disappointed.

"It makes one wonder," he went on bitterly, "just what the British Merchant Marine is coming to, when they license some overhauled ferryboat like the *Sunderland*, and call it a cruise ship. And put a clown like that Manley-Norville on as captain! Couldn't properly run a collier on the Tyne, in my opinion! And did you notice?" he added querulously. "They had the utter gall to fly the Union Jack, instead of the skull-and-crossbones! With those prices!"

Clifford Simpson merely puffed on his cigar and smiled gently. Simpson, after knowing Briggs — as the newspaper article had noted in one of its extremely few correct statements — for over five decades, had become accustomed to the other's tendency to exaggerate. Simpson was a very tall man, roughly twice the height of his companion, and almost painfully thin, who went through life with a constant expression of wonder on his slightly horselike face, as if silently marveling at the foibles of this earth of ours. He looked, in general, like a perpetually pondering pipe-cleaner, usually dressed in fuzzy tweed.

"Come now, Tim," he said in a rather amused, quite reasonable tone of voice, waving his Corona-Corona gently as he spoke, "the S.S. *Sunderland* is considered the finest British cruise ship afloat. Its captain is considered England's finest mariner. The fact that we got ourselves kicked off the ship by getting ourselves into trouble — "

"You mean because *I* was getting into trouble, don't you?" Briggs demanded belligerently.

"As you say," Simpson said, agreeing. Clifford Simpson was one of those men with the unfortunate habit of honesty. He shrugged elaborately and brushed ash into an ashtray on the table. "After all, dousing yourself with perfume and painting yourself with lip-rouge and pretending you were having a blazing affair with that poor girl aboard ship — and expecting to be believed, at your age! If it hadn't been for the services of Sir Percival Pugh — "

"Pugh!" Briggs made it sound like a homophone. It was the one name above all others guaranteed to raise the small man's hackles. "That twister! That thief! That penny-pinching miser! If he were a pot I'd bet he'd call the kettle collect! Not that he isn't a pot, mind you," Briggs added, thinking about it. "If it hadn't been for Pugh we'd never have been on the bloody boat in the first place!"

Clifford Simpson stared at his companion through the smoke of his cigar. Even for Tim Briggs, this was a bit much.

9

"Come, now, Tim!" he said in a tone that attempted to bring some degree of reason into the conversation. "Do you mean to say that if it hadn't been for Pugh's intervention when I was charged — quite accurately, as we both know — with murder, we might never have won the Jarvis award? And thereby been able to afford the cruise?" Simpson shook his head reprovingly. "Really, Tim! How convoluted can a person's thinking get? Even yours?"

"What I meant was — " Briggs began, and then stopped. He actually had no idea of what he meant. It was merely that to mention Sir Percival Pugh to Tim Briggs was like waving a copy of *The Worker* at a Tory. But he was saved the necessity of explaining himself, because at that moment the third member of the triumvirate that had won the Jarvis G-L-H-N-M Foundation award the previous year — as well as comprising the now-defunct Murder League — arrived. He was puffing a bit from his climb up the hill.

William Carruthers — Billy-Boy to his friends — was a rotund, cherubic-looking man with exceedingly bright china-blue eyes set in a round face beneath a halo of pure white hair. Billy-Boy Carruthers looked like a Kewpie doll that had been allowed to weather over too long a period of time; he looked the sort of perfect stranger that doting mothers would entrust their little babies to before ducking into a pub for a quick one. He might easily have played the part of an American senator on stage or screen, if an American senator could be pictured as benign, or as wearing a suit of a particularly nauseating shade of mustard yellow.

He seated himself with the other two, tapped the table significantly to draw the attention of a rather languorous waiter more interested in snapping a napkin at flies, waited until, at last, he had been furnished with a pony of brandy and a glass for the champagne, and then drank first the one after which he chased it with the other. These essentials of civilized conversation attended to, he burped gently, raised his eyes in the required apology, dabbed at his full lips with his handkerchief, tucked it back into his jacket sleeve, and beamed in genial fashion at his two companions.

"I have been to the airport," he announced. "In fact, I had the pleasure of seeing our good friend. Sir Percival, getting his ticket as well. He shall be on our flight, but he will travel first class, of course." He disregarded the *Grrraaagh* that came from Briggs at the hated name. "He sends his best, by the way."

"What he can do with his best — " Briggs began.

Carruthers disregarded this. Instead he tapped his breast pocket.

"I also picked up our tickets. Our flight is at one this afternoon. It will give us ample time to complete our packing and have a leisurely drink at the airport before departure. Luncheon will be served aboard the aircraft, I have been reasonably assured."

10

"At what price?" Briggs asked sourly.

"At no charge. You will also be both surprised as well as gratified, to learn that tipping is not only discouraged but is actually prohibited aboard aircraft."

"A pity the bloody *Sunderland* didn't have wings," Briggs said darkly, thinking back on the nicking their pocketbooks had taken in that regard aboard the vessel. He forced his mind from the unhappy memory of the voyage, in favor of more important business. He cleared his throat, trying to sound insouciant and almost succeeding. "Why don't I meet you two at the airport?"

Simpson looked up at him, surprised. "Aren't we all going down together?"

"I think I'll go ahead," Briggs said lightly, and came to his feet. "I'm all packed, you know. I'll just take my little airplane bag with me. I'd appreciate it if you could sling my other bag into the taxi with yours when you go down there." He saw the questioning look that remained on Simpson's face, and added a bit lamely, "I just want to do a little last minute sightseeing, you know. And possibly a little personal business." He raised a hand. "Ta, then. See you at the airport around one-ish. No need to get there too early, I suppose — "

Billy-Boy smiled at him gently.

"Sit down, Tim," he said quietly.

"But I've got this — "

"Sit down, Tim. There is no reason for any of us to get to the airport early, especially you."

"What do you mean?"

"I mean," Carruthers said with a faint smile, "that I've been through your airplane bag, and I'm afraid I had to remove several items. So why not sit down and relax?"

Briggs paled. He tried to bluster, but the words wouldn't come out. Simpson merely looked mystified, Carruthers turned to Simpson and explained. There was still a benign look on his pleasant, round face, and the smile remained on his lips, but the china-blue eyes were hard.

"Clifford," he said, "do you know what our small reprobate friend here was attempting to do? He had a small placard in his airplane bag, apparently purchased in one of the novelty shops here. It reads: OUT OF ORDER."

Simpson's look of bewilderment merely intensified. "Oh?"

"Yes. Our friend Briggs has also been visiting the airport," Carruthers went on coldly, "probably when we were napping. He has helped himself to some of those forms in the little box beside the contraption that dispenses air-insurance to any who wish it. Most of the forms, I imagine, if not all of them."

Simpson looked at Briggs in astonishment.

"Our larcenous friend was planning on attaching his sign to the insurance-vending machine. He then intended to sell the insurance to anyone who approached, wishing that service. He intended to use the proper form put out by the company, but instead of allowing the coins to go into the proper slot, of course, he intended to collect the fees himself. The only thing out of order is Timothy Briggs," Carruthers finished flatly. He turned to Briggs who was trying his best to look indignant at this violation of his privacy. "Tim, you utter idiot, have you considered what would happen if, perchance, the airplane might crash?"

"What?" Briggs asked defiantly.

"You know very well what! Bookmakers without proper funds to back them up probably furnish the River police with as much work dredging up their bodies as do paupers, or university students walking the Embankment railing after a night on the town!"

"You don't think I intended to countersign the bloody forms with my own name, do you?" Briggs exclaimed hotly. "Or put down my proper address?" He seemed more upset by the implied charge of stupidity than by having been caught.

"Still," Simpson said, having had time to digest what was occurring, "we'd be on the plane, too, so they could hardly hope to collect if it did crash, don't you see? I mean from Tim, of course."

While being incurably honest, Clifford Simpson was also logical. And while veracity was important to him, in his time he had been known to direct that honesty in advantageous ways. His conscience, in fact, would undoubtedly have caused any professor studying it to consider changing professions, or to babble.

"And if the plane didn't crash," Simpson went on, now caught up in the thing, "the passengers would have gotten their money's worth. The insurance company couldn't do any better than that for them, don't you see? If the plane didn't crash, that is." He puffed on his cigar while he thought a moment more, and then nodded. "It really isn't a bad idea at that, you know. If Tim got started right now, he could probably still get a few of them coming in to pick up their tickets — "

"Clifford, stop it! It's fraud," Carruthers said angrily.

"Of course," Simpson said, agreeing readily. "But we don't really know if the insurance company pays off either, do we? In case of a crash, I mean. After all, there are so few air accidents these days . . . . " His voice became dreamy with memory. "I remember I wanted to use insurance fraud in a story I wrote many years ago — not about airplanes, of course, since there were only a few Spads and Camels about at the time — but I really couldn't see what was so fictional about it, so I dropped the idea. I don't imagine insurance companies are any less fraudulent these days — "

Carruthers' large hand slammed down on the table, making their brandy glasses jump and causing a man at a nearby table, eating prawns with a toothpick, to stab himself painfully in the cheek. He looked at Carruthers reproachfully a moment and then forewent the toothpick to continue eating the prawns with his fingers.

"Now listen, you two reprobates," Carruthers said, keeping his voice down but using a tone the others knew meant Billy-Boy was not — as Clarence W. Alexander would have put it — playing potsie. "I believe I went through this entire routine once before for you, aboard the *Sunderland*. There is to be an end to chicanery, do you understand? There is to be no more fiddling! I told you before of that fine American author who lost a book-club sale of an accounting of our activities in the Murder League because we were naughty. Should that same fine and worthy American writer at any time in the future put into print our adventures since then, would you wish to deprive him of a possible book-club sale, through the needless repeating of our errors? As ex-writers ourselves, would that be cricket?"

Briggs stared at him in amazement.

"We commit ten murders," he said unbelievingly, "we push people from underground platforms — "

"We did, didn't we?" Simpson said, remembering, and added his bit. "We tossed them over hotel railings — "

"We poison their beer — " Briggs went on.

"We cosh them with soap bars wrapped in washcloths," Simpson said, getting into the spirit of the thing.

"We push fish slices in their throats, we drop them down elevator shafts," Briggs went on, "and you cavil at selling insurance to a bunch of blokes who ought to know better than to risk their lives flying in the first place — ?"

"Tim may be right," Simpson said thoughtfully. "Think of all the money you and I took from those card sharpers on board the *Sunderland*, Billy-Boy. I know at the moment you claimed it was all right because it was merely the biter-bit ploy, but — " He shrugged.

"Money we didn't even get to keep," Briggs said bitterly. "That so-called captain impounded it for evidence, and that was the last we saw of it! And as for that bloody, blithering, blaggedy blister of a bleary American writer — !" he added hotly.

"Enough!" Carruthers raised his hand over the table again, but lowered it in deference to the suddenly cringed shoulders of the prawn-eater, watching defensively from the corner of his eye. "There will be no further discussion," Carruthers said quietly but firmly. "Our investments in the Namibian Chartered Mines" — he tapped the money belt about his middle that contained the certificates of the shares, for Carruthers had not trusted banks since he had investigated them in 1922 for a book he was doing entitled *Vaulted Vultures* — "give us sufficient returns to handle our meager needs.

There is no necessity for doing anything not completely legitimate. From now on we will live the easy and blameless lives men our age are supposed to live. I myself shall probably take up the growing of roses. I would suggest daisies for you, Tim, as they grow closer to the ground. And possibly sunflowers for you, Cliff."

He drew a pocket watch from the depths of a vest pocket of his bilious suit and consulted it. His eyes came up.

"And now I suggest we begin gathering together our effects. We should not care to miss a final libation at the airport before embarking. And when we do, we shall toast" — he paused for a stern look at his two companions — "we shall drink to an end to malfeasance, at least on our part. For one thing, we're too old. We shall toast the start of the peaceful, the relaxed, the rewarding life . . . . "

3

"I don't get it, Clare," Harold said, puzzled. "We ask the old men to come and visit us? Here at the farm? Why?"

"Because I say so."

"Yeah, but I mean, why would they come?" Harold suddenly smiled, exhibiting teeth like polished sugar cubes. The dentist who had done the job, even Harold had to admit, had been an artist; it was simply that Harold's reaction upon receiving the bill had been automatic and had led, first, to his most recent term for assault and battery, and finally to his joining Clarence in his exile. "I ain't complainin', though," he added, not wishing to be misunderstood. "I kinda like the idea. I ain't never had a father, you know."

Clarence did not take the time to point out the physical improbability of this statement.

"Not all the old men," he said with a patience that was beginning to wear thin. He had a feeling he was repeating himself. "Just one of them."

"One at a time, you mean, Clare? Hey, that would be nice!" Harold suddenly frowned. "Only they always stick together, it said in the papers — "

"Not one at a time. Just the one of them. For just the one visit," Clarence said, trying not to grit his teeth. His teeth were the material of nature, and not

15

the plastic masterpieces that graced Harold's gums, and he knew that gritting them could lead to problems later in life. Still, it was difficult to refrain from grinding them. There were times when Clarence wished he had been more selective in his choice of associates. Certainly Harold's chief attribute, that of brute strength, would be of small use in the present caper; an eight-year-old girl with two broken arms, Clarence felt, should be able to handle any one of the three old men, if not all three together. At the moment what he wished he had was an associate with a little more imagination, plus a little more toughness, because Clarence had a feeling if he explained his true plan, Harold might object. And the kidnaping, as Clarence saw it, required two men if it were to be successful. Not that he felt Harold would object to kidnaping in principle; only where these particular three old men were concerned. It was, Clarence thought, what came of never having had a father.

Clarence had decided on kidnaping for several reasons. One, it was a crime almost unknown in England as far as he could determine, and the constabulary precautions against such malfeasance were therefore undoubtedly relatively debile, although it is doubtful he would have expressed it in exactly those words. Two, if the three old men really sacrificed everything each for the other à la Dumas' musketeers, as the newspapers claimed, then they certainly would not let a small matter of money stand between one of them and his freedom, or even his health, if it came to that. And lastly, kidnaping had a simplicity about it that Clarence admired in any scheme; it required no equipment and small expense, other than a little food for a few days.

Clarence had already taken most of the preliminary steps to assure a minimum of difficulties in the execution of the plan; he had already informed their sleep-out help, a certain Mrs. Southington, that Harold had come down with a virulent case of tertiary morosis which was highly contagious, and that it would be safer if she remained away until further notice. He had also laid in a goodly supply of food, including many pounds of tea, which he was sure would be necessary sustenance for an English old man. The problem, however, was to break the basic idea of the kidnaping to Harold without the big man getting the feeling that he would be, in essence, sequestering his own unknown father in surrogate.

"Hey, Clare," Harold said suddenly, hitting himself on the forehead for not having thought of it sooner, and instantly rubbing the injured spot, for he had a hand like the bumper on a gravel truck, "I got a great idea!"

"Yes," Clarence said absently, and went on checking off the points of his plan in his mind. He had already seen to it that their car, rented by the month at the cheapest rate possible — for though Clarence had money and was willing to expend a portion of it to further any scheme that could bring back a buck, he did not throw it away — had been properly filled with fuel;

he had made sure there were sufficient bedclothes and blankets around, as it would be counterproductive to let the old man die of pneumonia, at least until they collected the ransom. He ticked the points off in his head and then nodded to himself. The essentials had been met; the only thing left was to figure out some way to get Harold to go along with the scheme without being aware of his role until it was too late to back out. That would take a bit more thinking, but there was still an hour or so before the car had to leave to meet the flight from Gibraltar, and if he, Clarence, couldn't think of a way to confuse Harold in that span of time, then he promised himself to retire and take up honest labor.

"Yeah!" Harold said with enthusiasm, unaware that he had lost his audience. "Why don't we just snatch one of them old men?"

"Yes," Clarence said without consciously hearing a word. Maybe if he told Harold the old geezer was really a long-lost relative, an uncle, maybe, on his grandfather's side, only the old geezer didn't know it and he didn't want to spring it on him too suddenly, as old geezers notably had weak hearts — no, that didn't sound as if it could pass even with Harold —

"Hey, Clare, you ain't listening!" Harold sounded aggrieved. "I said I just had me a great idea. Why don't we simply put the old snatcheroo on one of the old — "

"Yes," Clarence said, and pressed his brain for a decent answer. Possibly if he told Harold he needed the old man's help in figuring out the plot of one of the old mysteries in the Avery farm library — after all, according to that Sunday supplement all three of them had once been mystery writers — he suddenly looked up, startled. "What did you say?"

"I said, why don't we just snatch one of them? Keep him here for a while," Harold said, waving one of his hamlike hands around as if in explanation. "We wouldn't hurt him. Just keep him here awhile." He might have been speaking of a pet rabbit, or a turtle.

Clarence studied the earnest features of his large confederate for several moments, wondering when he would learn not to prejudge people. It was a dangerous habit for a professional con man to get into. Maybe he had been in England too long; the damp weather, possibly, was beginning to warp his brain.

"Are you suggesting," he said slowly, "that we hold one of those poor old men for ransom? That's against the law, you know."

Harold waved this argument away as being specious.

"What ain't?" he demanded. "Sure we hold him for ransom; that gives us a good excuse to have him here, don't you see? They got lots of loot, it says in the papers, and I could sure use some. You got all the dough we got between us, but I'm broke. What do you say, Clare? It's a good idea, ain't it? We'd split the dough right down the line. What do you say? Huh?"

17

Clarence Wellington Alexander scratched his chin; it was the same sort of delaying come-on he used when people appeared eager to buy small amounts of oil-well stock, rather than the large, economy-sized blocks he preferred to sell.

"I don't know — "

"Sure it's a good idea!" Harold said fiercely. It was not often that ideas struck him, but he knew a good one when it did, and he hated to see it abandoned. "Look, Clare — I'll even do most of the work. You want one of them old men here, how do you expect to get him to come? Just by askin'? Maybe he says no. Maybe he don't like it on a farm; it took me a while, and I still ain't sure. I tell you, snatchin' one of them is the only way! I could pick him up at the airport when they come in, I bet! Bring him right out here. No sweat!" His mind, now as firmly in the saddle as it ever got, was charging along in all directions.

"Well, possibly — "

"No possibly. It's a sure thing." It was said with cold finality. It was rare, indeed, that Harold found himself this forceful with Clarence — without, that is, having his head handed to him verbally. It was an intoxicating feeling. "And it was lucky you went shoppin' yesterday; we got enough food in the joint to last weeks." He frowned as a snag in his scheme suddenly appeared. "There's one thing, though. What about that old bag who comes in to do the cleanin'?"

"Mrs. Southington?" Clarence shook his head at the tragedy that besets even the best of us in this cruel world. "Poor soul, she's pretty sick. She came down with shrinking edema, I just learned yesterday. She won't be able to come in for a week or so."

"See?" Harold came as close to crowing as his gravel voice would allow. It was almost as if the gods were blessing the venture. "It all works out! I tell you, Clare, it's a natural!" He could not imagine how any rational person could doubt the rightness of the idea, and therefore moved on to the next point, hoping that sheer momentum would bring Clare into camp. "Which one of them are we goin' to snatch, Clare?"

"Which one would you prefer for company?" Clarence asked, now feeling generous.

Harold was delighted with himself; his ploy had worked. He closed his eyes and tried to recall the newspaper article with its accompanying photograph. When he finally brought it into focus, he examined it carefully. He nodded.

"The fat guy, I think," he said, and opened his eyes, blinking. "Yeah. He looks like the happiest one, like he'd be the most fun. And also, them fat guys can't run so fast, if he gets any funny ideas." He suddenly grinned; it looked as if someone had opened a new box of pipless dice. "Hey! We're really goin' to do it, Clare?"

"Well," Clarence said, finally allowing himself to be sold, "all right. If you think you can snatch him at the airport and bring him back here without any fuss" — Harold snorted at the thought of any old man, or any ten of them together, giving him any trouble — "and," Clarence added, "without half of the airport seeing you and following you." He studied Harold. "Can you do it?"

"Sure!" Harold said expansively, and then paused. Faced with the need to consider the minute details, his mind stumbled to its normal halt. The basic idea was sound, he was convinced, but unfortunately, that was as far as he had gone.

Clarence, watching the uncertainty take over from the assured on Harold's face, took pity on the big man.

"You know," he said pensively, as if the idea had just occurred to him and had not been conceived hours before, "I'll bet if I were to be at the airport, too, and somehow managed to separate the fat man from the other two, all you would have to do would be to take charge of him, get him into the car, and be on your way."

"Yeah!" Harold said, overwhelmed by the profundity of Clarence's solution. He had been sure that once Clarence had accepted the basic premise, he would contribute his share to the success of the venture. A rift, though, appeared in the lute. "Only how you goin' to get the fat man alone by hisself?"

"I'll think of something," Clarence promised, and went back to his original idea. "When you have him in the car, tell him you were sent to pick him up by some company — say a television company — to take him someplace for an interview. He'll go quietly enough. Tell him his two friends will meet him later." He nodded in satisfaction as the final pieces fell into place. "Yes, that should do it nicely. Tell him his friends will meet him at his club, that Mystery Writers thing the paper mentioned. String the story out as long as he isn't suspicious, but if he starts to get the idea that something isn't kosher in Kankakee, that he's being snatched — "

"Yeah? What then, Clare?"

Clarence eyed the large man coldly. "Then you just have to make sure he stays quiet the rest of the way."

"Oh. Sure." Harold nodded automatically, and then checked himself. "But I ain't goin' to hurt him, am I, Clare? Because I don't really want to hurt him, Clare."

"Nobody is going to hurt anyone," Clarence said soothingly. "We're just going to have a guest for a few days. A paying guest," he added significantly, and smiled.

"A what?" Harold pondered. Suddenly his dazzling smile appeared, to be followed by what would have been an anguished growl from a dog suffering a bone in its throat, but with Harold was a guffaw. "A payin' guest, huh, Clare? Hey, that's good."

"Yes," Clarence said, and glanced at his watch. "And now, if you'll get the car out, we'll be on our way. Luckily, between here and the airport is largely open country; you won't have to put up with city traffic." Or too many curious people, he thought, who might wonder at seeing a fat man struggling with a giant in what even the Japanese would have called a small car. "You drop me at the nearest telephone booth to the arrival building," he continued, "and then go around to where they come out of customs. I'll see to it that the fat one is alone when he comes through. You pick him up and bring him back here and entertain him until I come back."

"You ain't comin' with us, Clare?"

"No. I'll go into town from the airport and take a train from there and a taxi from the station to come home when I'm through. Besides, three's a crowd — " In their small English car two would have been a crowd. "And I have other things to do."

"Like what, Clare? Huh?" Harold's brow was furrowed, his tone plaintive. "You ought to tell me what you're goin' to do, Clare. After all, snatchin' the old man was my idea in the first place, you want to remember."

"I shall never forget it," Clarence said soothingly. "What I shall be doing is first composing the ransom note, and then dropping it in the mail. That's a basic move in all kidnapings, you know."

"Oh. Yeah. Sure, I forgot," Harold said.

"And another basic thing in kidnaping," Clarence went on, "is to make sure your captive has no idea where he is being held. So when you get near the farm, make sure you blindfold him. Understand?"

"Oh, sure."

"And another of the usual procedures is to make sure your victim doesn't walk out of the door when you turn your back, or go to the john, or something. When you have him inside, handcuff him to something, a chair or a bed. Understand?"

"Sure," Harold said, almost disdainfully. He had seen as many snatch movies as the next guy, and more than Clare, he bet. Then he frowned. "Only I ain't got any handcuffs."

"Then tie him up, or sit on him, I don't care which. Just make sure he's still there when I get back."

"Oh. Sure." He suddenly grinned. "Hey, Clare, how much we goin' to ask for him, huh, Clare?"

"That's another thing I have to do in town," Clarence said. "I shall also be determining the size of the award they received. A phone call to a newspaper ought to handle that, I imagine."

"We ain't goin' to ask for all of it, are we, Clare?" Harold said in a worried tone. "We don't want to leave them broke. We don't want no old men to starve, do we, Clare?"

"If the award they got is as big as it sounded," Clarence said, "half should do nicely." He looked at his watch and then up at Harold significantly.

"I get you," Harold said. At times he could exhibit almost human intelligence. "You mean you want to leave now, Clare?"

"If we're going to leave at all," Clarence said rather pointedly.

He watched the huge man leave the farmhouse and walk lumberingly toward the barn that served as their garage. Clarence was still not quite sure how he had conned Harold into believing the kidnaping was his idea, and it bothered Clarence a bit not to be able to pinpoint the exact words he had said that had triggered the desired response in Harold's brain. It might have proved useful in some future con. Still, he supposed it didn't really matter. Like his namesake in the matter of the sunken road at Waterloo, C. Wellington A. was not one to look a gift horse in the mouth.

4

light No. 129 from Gibraltar's North Front airport to Heathrow in London made the passage quite routinely, with no skyjacking, no illegal sale to passengers of duty-free brandy and champagne purchased in Gibraltar, no filching of soap, or towels, or electric razors from the aircraft's washrooms — or, for that matter, any last-minute flight insurance forms being hawked in the aisles. The reason for the absence of these transgressions, at least to the mind of Billy-Boy Carruthers, was that he had placed Briggs in the window seat on the right-hand side of the 707 jet, had located Simpson in the middle despite the crowded condition suffered by his legs and knees, and had plugged the outlet by seating his almost eighteen stone on the aisle.

But he really need not have worried. Briggs, on his first flight ever, was completely enthralled by the view and kept his bright little eyes glued to the window, while Simpson, also on his first flight, with his greater height was easily able to crane over Briggs and also enjoy the view. And, in time — as these things happen — they had come in over the mouth of the Thames and were flying lower and lower over the heart of the great city, with the broad river snaking its way beneath them, directing them generally to the west and the airport somewhere in that direction. Suddenly Briggs pointed.

"Hoy! Right there! The club!"

He could not, of course, actually see the small building where the Mystery Authors Club was located, since it was hidden behind a huge insurance company building which had been erected after the founding of the club and which now interjected itself between their tiny edifice and Swan's Park. But the park itself was easily distinguishable, as well as the large electric sign atop the insurance company, offering wondrous benefits to any policyholder sufficiently avaricious as to die; double if he did so painfully in an accident.

Carruthers, denied the view but preferring his role as the stopper in the bottle, smiled as he saw the club in his mind's eye. The three of them had founded the mystery writers' organization more years before than he cared to remember, and he could picture the northeast corner of the club's lounge where the three worn but comfortable arm chairs were located, flanked by small tables capable of holding — now that they could afford it — their brandy and champagne glasses, and their beer mugs in those past days when they could not. It was a protective alcove safe from the inane chatter of the younger members, and the intrusive presence of Potter, the secretary. In a short while Carruthers supposed the three of them would be there, leaving their luggage temporarily in the custody of the hall porter, and settling down for the remainder of the day before going their respective ways in the evening, each taking his bags with him, to face another lonely night, each in his own small rooms.

His smile faded. Seen in that light, the prospect was not exactly enchanting. In a way Tim Briggs was right. It was rather sad, after all the adventures they had enjoyed over the past months, to return to the dullness and purpose-lessness that had characterized their previous existence. While he could not condone Briggs's attempted ploy with the insurance forms, he could understand it. Still, what could be done? They were not getting any younger, and that was an even sadder fact. And there were undoubtedly younger and more ambitious miscreants around London in greater need of illegal funds, for at least the three of them were fortunate enough not to be suffering the penury that had been their unfortunate lot before the Murder League and the unexpected Jarvis award had freed them from poverty's clutches.

With this slender fact to give him what little cheer he could garner from it, Carruthers picked up the journal that had been handed him when his luncheon tray had been removed, and prepared to while away the final moments of the flight in the educational pursuit of reading and catching up on the news. He noted the headlines, bit back a yawn, and turned the page.

And received the greatest shock of his life.

Their stocks had crashed! Their investments were worthless!

Carruthers gripped the newspaper tightly while he read the story. The Namibian Chartered Mines, Ltd., according to the article, while basically as honest as most gold-mining companies, had had the misfortune of running out of the product which they had been formed to exploit. That vein of the precious yellow stuff which the entrepreneurs had hired others to excavate had inexplicably disappeared, and had there been value in barren rock they might have survived, but since this was not the case, the company had only sympathetic noises to make to their unfortunate shareholders. A penny on a pound, it was estimated by the director being quoted, might eventually be realized in liquidation, but it could not be promised.

Carruthers read the article a second and then a third time, wetting his lips, his hand unconsciously stroking the bulge that represented the money belt and the now worthless stock certificates. But no amount of repetition could alter the tragic facts. He glanced quickly over at his two friends. They were still intent upon the rapidly foreshortening view, this one gleefully pointing out that, that one merrily pointing out this, and generally acting as Columbus had probably acted upon sighting the New World. Should he reveal the disastrous news to them now, and ruin the small pleasures they were relishing at the moment? No, he thought sadly; they'll know in time enough!

He sighed mightily. Back to poverty! No more brandy and champagne; back to beer, and probably some slop brewed within the past few hours, tasting as it did just after the war! No more fine lunches; back to cucumber sandwiches with the cucumbers sliced wafer thin by sniffling girls in shops with soiled napery, watercress salads produced by herb-pinching misers; and back to the malevolent and accusatory looks from tipless waiters and waitresses! No more vacation trips — although he was forced to admit that Briggs, for one, would probably cut his legs off at the knees before he took another cruise. But that wasn't the point. The point was — no more almost anything!

He tried to look at it philosophically. The stock certificates were certainly colorful, and there was that stain on the wall of his room he had been meaning to cover with a picture for some years now. A few of the shares, properly framed, would do the job nicely, and he would be surprised if Briggs and Simpson, using their imaginations, could not also find an equally useful outlet for their certificates. Besides, of what benefit was crying over spilt milk? After all, they were no worse off than they had been a few months back. Still, that had been no bed of roses, so there was little consolation in that thought. Possibly he should not have objected when Briggs wanted to sell that airplane insurance; it simply proved that one never knew in this world. And as for that idiot American author, what did they owe him? It might, in fact, even teach the moron to be a little more sure of his facts before he put his inanities to paper.

He sighed again moodily and tightened his seat belt as the sign went on above his head. Poor Tim and poor Cliff, he thought, and lurched forward gently as the plane touched down.

24

If Assistant Commissioner of Police Horace Winterblast was not particularly famous for his contribution to the law and order of the area supposedly under his jurisdiction, he was, none the less, quite well known through the British Isles. Scarcely a week went by without the florid face of A.C. Horace Winterblast being seen on one or more television programs. On news programs he was usually explaining why perpetrators had not been apprehended; on talk shows those deep, well-recognized nasal tones easily balanced any humor that might have been attempted by an invited comic. On public service programs Winterblast could be guaranteed to come up with some homily about the hard-working police — although many suspected he would need a map to find his own office, so seldom was he there — while on game shows he usually sat as one of the panel of judges, eyeing each contestant malevolently, as if he were a criminal, or — far worse — a candidate for the A.C.'s job.

So pervasively intrusive was Assistant Commissioner Winterblast in the everyday life of most Englishmen, that it never occurred to customs officer James J. Griggsby to be surprised to hear the familiar voice on the telephone, or to be curious as to why Winterblast was calling him, or even to wonder at the omniscience of the A.C.'s intelligence service.

"Winterblast here! You will act immediately!" the familiar voice was saying with its normal callous authority. "Immediately, do you hear? Most blatant case of smuggling I ever heard of! Diamonds, drugs, animal skins — !"

It was with an effort that Clarence restrained himself. He had a tendency to get carried away with his impersonations. He got back on the track and carried on.

"Two scoundrels, a short miscreant named Timothy Briggs and a tall thin one called Clifford Simpson! Traveling with a man named Carruthers, but he's quite all right, yes, quite all right. Wouldn't touch him, you know, under any circumstances, related to Lord Hummmmohhh, I once heard. But the others, this Briggs and this Simpson, shouldn't be surprised if they weren't aliases. Yes. Hummmmph! Arriving on Flight 129 from Gib, that's Gib, you hear? Should be coming in any minute now, I should imagine." The voice suddenly paused and then came back on, highly accusative. "Are you listening to me, sir?"

"Yes, sir. Oh, yes, sir, I am!"

"I was beginning to wonder. All right, get on with it then, son. But you understand, no fuss! No fuss, you understand!" The voice became querulous. "You do understand, don't you?"

Customs officer Griggsby did *not* understand.

"I beg your pardon, sir? No fuss?"

"Exactly!" The booming nasal voice sounded pleased at the other's instant grasp of the situation. "Glad you see it my way, son. No sense inviting a lot of publicity about these things, eh? What? Give people ideas, eh? What? No, just take those two someplace, into a private office or something, and give them the business, eh? Take them apart, what? Top to bottom, turn them upside down and shake them, pockets inside out and things like that, eh? What? But it's not for me to tell a man how to do his job. Not even my department, customs, eh? But we're all Englishmen and loyal to the Queen, what? Just see that it's done, eh? What?"

"Yes, sir! Right away, sir!"

"Good-o! Hummmph! By the way, what's your name, son?"

"James — er — Griggsby, sir."

"James R. Grizzly. I shall not forget this. Grizzly! Now, do your duty!"

"Oh yes, sir, I shall, I shall," Griggsby began to say, but he was protesting his intended efficiency to a dial tone. He hung up and turned to the small computerized television screen on his desk; at the moment he would not have been surprised to see the familiar florid features of Assistant Commissioner Horace Winterblast glaring at him from the flickering screen for wasting time. But what he actually saw was the schedule of arriving and departing planes, and he was pleased to see that Flight 129 from Gibraltar had just landed and was even now trundling its way to the unloading area.

Plenty of time, he thought, and smiled to himself as he reached for the telephone again. All it took was one break, he thought. With luck A.C. Winterblast might even get him a spot on one of the more lucrative game shows. If he did the job right, of course, and James J. Griggsby had no intention of not doing the job to perfection.

The three elderly friends filed from the plane with the other passengers. They climbed aboard the waiting bus, each with his own thoughts, and climbed down at the Immigration building, the newspaper with the tragic news tucked under Carruthers' arm. They formed up in the obligatory queues at the obligatory windows, had the obligatory stamps pressed onto their passports by the obligatorily sour-faced personnel after the obligatory delays, and made their way into the luggage-claim area, paying small attention to the loud-speaker that was blaring above their heads. Suddenly Simpson paused. Either because his mind was less occupied, or because his extreme height brought him closer to the noisy diaphragms suspended from the ceiling, he seemed to recognize at least a portion of the words, which was rather remarkable, considering airport acoustics.

"I say," he said wonderingly. He had been in the process of lighting the remains of his Corona-Corona which he had obediently stubbed out at the exhortation of the sign above their seats upon landing. He shook out the match and tucked the cigar into his breast pocket. "I do believe they are referring to us — ?"

26

"Us?" Briggs said truculently, and tilted his head back to stare distrustfully at the cloth-covered boxes spouting sounds from above. "That's right," he said, frowning darkly. "They're paging you and me, Cliff. Why just the two of us? Why not Billy-Boy, too?"

"It's probably nothing to worry about," Carruthers said, but in a worried tone. Could it be, he wondered, that some ill-wisher — Potter, the club secretary, possibly — could not wait for the newspaper story to reach them regarding the failure of Namibian Chartered Mines, Ltd., but wished to get in first with the dire news? But that was impossible. Other than the three of them, nobody knew what they had invested in. And Potter would certainly have aimed his poisoned dart at all three of them, not just two. "It's probably just the Journals again," he suggested, "or the S.S. *Sunderland* offices wishing an endorsement. You go along." It seemed as good a time as any to share the bad news; they could not be kept in the dark forever. "And take this along," he said sadly, handing the newspaper to Simpson. "Page two."

"Right-o," Simpson said agreeably, and tucked the paper into his pocket. He reached out a long arm to tap the shoulder of an uniformed figure hurrying through the area. Customs officer Griggsby turned around, saw the short man beside the tall, thin man, made a rapid calculation in his brain, linking the two to the noises from the loudspeaker he himself had initiated, and beamed.

"You are Clifford Simpson?"

"That's right," Simpson said, somewhat baffled by the instant recognition, but somewhat pleased by it as well.

"And this, I gather, is Timothy Briggs?"

"That's bloody well too-damn right!" Briggs said belligerently. "Now; what's this all about?"

"A private word with you two gentlemen, if you please," Griggsby said with a tone of politeness he was sure A.C. Winterblast would have admired. It was the tone he would use, he decided, it he ever got on "Noughts-and-Squares"; then the panel worked with you and not against you. "In my office?"

"And what about our luggage?" Briggs demanded.

"You'll find it waiting for you there," Griggsby said significantly.

He waited with anticipation for the shocked and/or frightened look of criminals-unmasked to cross the two faces, but all he got was a look of complete bewilderment from the tall, horse-faced one, and an angry glare of impatience from the short, peppery one. In all his years of experience, James J. Griggsby had come across some hard cases, but these two were undoubtedly the most calloused smugglers he had ever encountered. Not the slightest sign of guilt crossed their visages. For the briefest of moments James J. Griggsby wondered if possibly the assistant commissioner could have made a mistake, but this, he knew, was impossible. No, these two were simply rascals more clever than most. They probably figured their advanced age would permit them to pass Her Majesty's Customs without suspicion. Well, little did they reck! He cleared his throat authoritatively.

"All right," he said firmly, and remembered Winterblast's admonition. "And no fuss, either! Come along, now."

"Wait a moment," Carruthers said, suddenly getting into the act. This certainly had nothing to do either with interviews from journals, nor with their losing their money. He looked at Briggs sternly. "Tim, tell the truth. What mischief did you get into in Gibraltar before we left that I know nothing about?"

"Who, *me*?" Briggs said in a semi-shriek, highly incensed. "Nothing, I swear!"

"Cliff?"

"Yes, Billy-Boy?" Simpson smiled at his friend in comradely fashion, and then suddenly understood the question. "Oh! You mean, what mischief did *I* get into?" He pondered a moment and then nodded. "None, I'm quite positive. Clean as a church mouse."

"That's poor," Carruthers said, and almost added, like us. He put the bitter thought aside and turned to the customs officer. "Then I'm afraid, sir, that I must ask you for an explanation."

"And I'm afraid I must refuse to give you one," Griggsby said flatly. "You're Mr. Carruthers, aren't you? Well, sir, you are not involved, and if you want my suggestion, you will not get yourself involved!"

Carruthers was about to challenge that statement when, to his utter astonishment, little Tim Briggs began to giggle. The others also considered him with surprise.

"It's all right, Billy-Boy," Briggs said, and winked. "I get it, now. You go ahead. We'll see you later at the club." As Carruthers continued to stare, Briggs leaned toward him, covering his mouth, whispering. "It's that Candid Camera thing, don't you see? What else could it be? And they give out prizes, you know . . . . " He straightened up with another wink.

As Briggs marched off confidently beside Simpson, with customs officer Griggsby hurrying to catch up, Billy-Boy watched his taller friend take the newspaper from his pocket and start to turn the page to the financial news on page two. Carruthers turned away before any anguished cries could reach his ears. If only it *were* Candid Camera, he thought disconsolately, with the prize a lifetime supply of good food as well as brandy and champagne. For three, of course . . . .

28

But he knew it wasn't.

Sir Percival Pugh, also approaching the luggage-claim area, but unseen or at least unnoted by the three, frowned slightly to see Timothy Briggs and Clifford Simpson being cut away from the herd by a man who was obviously a customs official. Sir Percival's massive brain instantly went into action. It was extremely doubtful that the two had managed to get into trouble on the airplane, even though Sir Percival would have been the last to deny their ability to get into trouble in a reasonably short period of time. Someone had therefore either made a mistake, or the customs official had been diddled for the purpose of separating Carruthers from his two friends. While mistakes by customs officials were certainly not uncommon, they were not overwhelming, and Sir Percival was a great believer in the percentages. In this case, therefore, he felt fairly confident that the customs official had been used as a pawn to allow Billy-Boy Carruthers to emerge from the building unaccompanied by his two friends.

His mammoth intelligence having gone this far, Sir Percival went on to consider the long face he had noted on Carruthers as opposed to the rather cheerful expression on the faces of the other two at the moment of parting. Since Carruthers had been the blithest of spirits just that morning, and had even been seen smiling brightly at the moment of embarkation onto Flight 129, Pugh could only assume he had received bad news since then. But what bad news could possibly have been transmitted to just one of the triumvirate without the other two having been informed as well? Undoubtedly something Carruthers had read on the airplane and had not cared to disturb the other two with, while they were enjoying the flight. And the only bad news in the paper handed out on the plane had been the failure of the Namibian Chartered Mines, Ltd.

It was now all clear. The three had put their money from the Jarvis award into the shares of Namibian, and were now broke, but Simpson and Briggs were as yet unaware of the fact.

Sir Percival Pugh, in addition to being a giant intellect, was also the finest criminal lawyer in all England. He was also the most successful; he had never lost a case. When "Killer" Kiley, the well-known bank robber and psychopathic murderer, was accused by reliable eyewitnesses of slaying six hostages in the course of stealing eleven thousand four hundred and eight pounds from the Millrace Bank in Upper Lowerly, Sir Percival was able to prove to the satisfaction of both jury and judge that the witnesses were suffering from mirage, caused by the light reflection from all the new notes, and that what appeared to be murder was actually the greatest mass suicide since Masada. Not only was Kiley acquitted, but Pugh was even able to have Kiley reimbursed for the ammunition expended, by the bereaved relatives of the deceased. His fee, by an odd coincidence, was exactly eleven thousand four hundred and eight pounds.

For Sir Percival loved money. But since at the moment he could see no probable gain from three old men without funds, no matter how enjoyable the mental exercise of considering their predicament might be, he put the matter out of mind and went on to practice his basic philosophy of patience and faith by moving to the luggage-arrival conveyor and waiting.

5

Had the designers of Heathrow Airport given sufficient thought to the possible use of their premises for the purposes of kidnaping, it is probable they would have been a bit more generous in directing both incoming victim and potential sequesterer to the same exit to make contact. As it was, the customs area discharged arriving passengers into a vast arena filled with screaming relatives, small children entangled in luggage carts, porters taking the incorrect baggage of the wrong parties to erroneous taxi-ranks, and with an overabundance of access openings. Harold Nishbagel, cruising slowly past the multiple doorways of the vast building, with constant streams of impatient humanity fighting their way past each other, was beginning to feel the first touches of panic as he realized the excellent possibility of missing his party. While not a person of outstanding imagination, Harold was still capable of easily picturing Clarence's reaction should he fail to appear at the farm with the fat man in attendance. It was not a scene he cared to dwell upon.

He was about to tread heavily on the accelerator and attempt to speed around the building for another pass at the seemingly endless crowded exits, when he saw to his vast relief a mustard-colored balloon-sized figure emerge from a doorway not too distant, taking with it in the process several small bodies intent upon entering, and make its way to the stop for city-bound buses. Without any overwhelming regard for intervening traffic, Harold aimed at the curb and sped for it, arriving just as the white-haired, blue-eyed gentleman was straightening up from setting down his single bag. Harold leaned over, swinging open the door on the passenger side of the car, then opening his own door and climbing down. The wildly honking horns occasioned by his rather abrupt passage across the busy thoroughfare prevented him from being heard at first, but once the exigencies of vehicular movement cleared the disgruntled motorists from the scene, he came through loud and clear.

"Hey! You there! You — fat man!" he called out, not wishing to be misunderstood. His brilliant plastic smile robbed the unconventional greeting of any offense. "I'm supposed to be pickin' you up. Hop in."

He opened the car's trunk and tossed Carruthers' bag inside, while Billy-Boy stared, surprised. A large hand next propelled the rotund, mustard-colored man around the car and managed to wedge him into the front seat before he could quite recover himself. When he did so he found his massive driver had squeezed himself into the other side of the small vehicle and was releasing the hand brake preparatory to launching them once again into the traffic pattern, if pattern properly describes the anarchy that appeared to prevail in the road.

From another exit, Sir Percival Pugh watched and frowned. The reason for the separation of the three friends had now become clear. Someone, undoubtedly unaware of the financial disaster that had overtaken the three old men, and probably relying solely on the information gained from that Sunday supplement in color, had come to the conclusion that kidnaping one of the three old men, in this case Carruthers, would be an easy road to riches.

Well, on their own heads be it, Sir Percival thought uncharitably of the kidnapers; whoever they are they'll be sadder and wiser men before they're through. And he raised his hand for a taxi.

In the small car, Carruthers was frowning at the driver.

"I beg your pardon," he said politely, "but I do believe you've made a mistake. Normal enough, of course. I realize I probably look like every other old, fat man with blue eyes and white hair, wearing a mustard-colored suit, but I'm afraid it's a mistake none the less. You see, I wasn't expecting to be picked up."

"No mistake, pops," Harold said cheerfully, and cut between a lorry loaded with concrete building blocks and a bus filled with Welsh footballers, all singing at the tops of their voices. From the little glimpse Harold had of them through the open windows of the bus, he could scarcely credit their vocal efforts; when he had played right tackle for Sing Sing, nobody sang after the mauling it appeared the bus passengers had taken. Crazy! Harold thought, and shook his head. England! He shrugged and brought his attention back to his passenger. "No mistake at all, pops," he said. "You're William Carruthers, ain't you?" He did not give Carruthers a chance to deny it. "I seen your picture in the paper."

"That's quite correct," Billy-Boy said, mystified by the affair. "Now, to complete this informative exchange of relative trivia, just who are you?"

"Me? My name's Harold Nishbagel, but you can call me Hal. Most people call me Hal," he added darkly, "on account of I tell them to. I like it better than Harold." He started to extend a hamlike hand across the car toward Carruthers to be shaken, but thought better of it as a tow truck dragging a crippled charabanc almost collided with them; with more luck than skill Harold swung the wheel and managed to avoid disaster. In Chicago, when he had lived and worked there, he had been trusted with many demanding tasks, but driving the getaway car had never been one of them.

Carruthers swallowed. "I say," he said tentatively, watching the scenery swirl about him as Harold straightened the wheels, "you haven't driven much in England, have you?"

"A guy would have to be crazy," Harold said fervently, and narrowly missed a double-decker whose driver was apparently more interested in the décolletage of a female passenger seen through his rear-view mirror than he was in the traffic. "They drive backward!"

"And you are an American." It was a statement, not a question.

Harold beamed. He hadn't known it showed. "Yeah!"

"Well," Carruthers said, wriggling in the tight seat in a vain effort to find a more comfortable position, "now that these niggling but undoubtedly vital facts are out of the way, could I inquire as to who requested you to pick me up? And precisely why? And, of course, to complete the catechism, the ultimate destination of our little outing as well as the estimated time of arrival?"

A single question was Harold's absolute limit; three or four at a time were far beyond his ability to cope. Billy-Boy saw the wrinkles beginning to form on Harold's brow, like hairline cracks forecasting the collapse of a concrete dam. He properly interpreted them and took pity on his large companion.

"Let's take them one at a time," he said gently, removing his gaze, not reluctantly, from the roadway unfolding before them, and turning instead to consider his driver. "First of all, to be succinct, what is this all about?"

Harold, at least, knew the answer to that one. "Television," he said promptly.

"Ah? We're on television?" Carruthers looked around; as he had suspected, they were not.

"Naw. They're goin' to interview you."

33

"Ah!" It didn't make much more sense, but at least it was intelligible and at this point every little bit helped. "And just who is going to so honor me?"

"All I know is television," Harold said, not about to be caught out so easily.

"Sorry," Carruthers said contritely. "Let us go on. I shall attempt another tack. Why are these so-discerning folks going to interview just me? What about my two friends?"

Harold knew the answer to this question, as well. He felt sure that Clarence would have been proud of the manner in which he was acquitting himself.

"Your friends are goin' to meet you later," he said in his gravel voice, and tried to remember what else Clarence had said. "Oh! Yeah. At your club. Somethin' about writin'."

It had long since occurred to Billy-Boy Carruthers that there was something odd, to say the very least, about the entire affair. While he knew relatively little about the operation of television studios, he was sure they were sufficiently sound financially to be able to afford better transportation for potential interviewees than the small, uncomfortable car in which he found himself. He also seemed to recall a recent article in the *Times* regarding the difficulty of foreigners obtaining work permits with the high unemployment, and it appeared doubtful to him that the hulk beside him could pass the liberal reading and spelling requirements, let alone the driving test. Nor did he think for a moment — as Timothy Briggs might have done — that they were merely in a segment of "Candid Camera"; for one thing the car was too small for people, let alone auxiliary photographic equipment, and if they were being filmed from another car it would have to be with telescopic sights, for by this time they were far from the airport and practically alone on the road.

Still, there had to be some real purpose in his having been selected and picked up at the airport. It was not impossible that there were two William Carrutherses in the world, but the giant beside him had seemed to recognize him, as well as know his name, and the giant had also stated that his two friends were to meet him at the club and had also known that the club had something to do with writin'. No, it appeared he was the William Carruthers referred to in the index, and the burning question was, why? Billy-Boy Carruthers had always been curious by nature, and the present problem intrigued him. Besides, as he had been thinking on the plane, life had promised to be dull, and this strange encounter — even should it eventually prove to be nothing more than a matter of mistaken identity, or a weird desire on someone's part to collect fat men named William Carruthers — should still provide conversational manna with his friends in the barren wilderness of the dull days ahead. He glanced from the car window and found confirmation of his growing suspicion that all was not as it should be.

"I say," he said a bit apologetically, "we're heading away from the city."

Harold had been prepared for this for some time and was proud to have thought of a good answer without Clarence's help.

"Short cut," he said succinctly.

"Obviously," Carruthers said, agreeing. "But where to?"

Harold swallowed. "Television — " he began, and then fell silent.

Carruthers frowned. It was highly dubious that there were any television studios on the road they were taking, much before Birmingham, if there. No, the television studio and the purported interview were tales, nothing more, and he was not unhappy about it. The bright lights would have made him blink for hours, and besides he suffered terribly from stage fright. But, then, what other reason could there possibly be for being here in this car with a driver whose conversation seemed to be largely limited to the word "television"? A possible — although highly improbable — explanation came to him. He looked at Harold speculatively.

"I say!" he said. "You wouldn't be kidnaping me, would you?"

Harold looked at him, startled, almost losing control of the car.

"You wasn't supposed to know about that until I got you at the farm!" He glanced swiftly at the road and then back again to the portly man beside him. "Don't go tellin' Clare that I said anythin', because I didn't! You guessed it yourself!"

"Clare?"

"Clarence."

"And just who is this Clarence?" Carruthers asked, always liking to keep track of the cast of characters.

"My partner. Well, he's really the boss," Harold admitted. Another thought came to the large man as he reviewed the damage done by Carruthers' lucky guess. "You ain't goin' to make a fuss, are you?"

"Fuss?" The question was patently puzzling. "Why should I make a fuss? And, to be truthful, being wedged in like this, exactly how would I go about making a fuss?"

"Good!" Harold said, greatly relieved. He would not have wanted to use muscle on the old man. Carruthers looked just as Harold had always hoped his father might have looked, rather than the front-view, side-view, post-office portrait his mother had kept on her dresser and which was as close as he had ever come to knowing his sire.

Kidnaped! Carruthers mused. In a way it was flattering. Not very many people his age had ever had the distinction of being kidnaped, and certainly very few people — if any at all — had been kidnaped who were in his financial straits. Then, like the thorough chap he always tried to be, he stopped to consider the other side of the coin. He eyed Harold with a touch of apprehension. The man was certainly large and rough-looking, and the denouement in some of the kidnapings he had read about had not always been sweetness and light.

"I say," he asked with a combination of curiosity and apprehension, "you wouldn't really harm me, would you?"

"Once your pals chip in, you'll be free as air, pops," Harold said positively. "What the hell — pardon me — but you and that midget Briggs did it for that Simpson guy, didn't you? I read all about it in the papers. So why shouldn't they do it for you?"

"Well, for one reason — " Billy-Boy began, and then realized that this was probably not the best time for financial confessions. "I gather," he said, changing the subject, returning to one more important in his mind, "that in that case I'm to be kept in reasonably fit condition?"

"Fit?" Harold asked, puzzled.

"I mean, you could scarcely expect my friends to pay for a dead man, could you? Not very much, at least."

"Dead? Who said anything about dead?" Harold asked, shocked. He knew, of course, that some unscrupulous snatchers polished off their victims even after being paid off, but he hoped that he himself was above such treachery, and particularly in the case of a sweet old man like the man beside him. "Don't worry your head about a thing, pops," he said reassuringly. "Not a thing."

As if to prove there was nothing to worry about in a mere case of kidnaping, Harold swung the wheel of the car, sending them from the highway into the lane leading to the farm barn, cutting ahead of a speeding cab-and-trailer, narrowly missing two bicyclists as he bumped over the curb, barely skirting two trees, and coming to a halt with the front wheels inches from the edge of a deep, water-filled ditch. He squeezed himself from the car and went around to open the other door for his guest.

"Made it!" he said triumphantly. "Well, here you are, pops, your home away from home for a couple of days." Suddenly he remembered something. "Hey! I forgot to blindfold you! Clare will have a fit! You wasn't supposed to see where you was at!"

Carruthers gazed about with a faint air of distaste. "I can understand why," he said, and then put himself in the large man's shoes. "However, I promise not to say anything if you don't."

"Hey, pops, that's swell of you," Harold said, beaming. Then his face fell. "I hate to do this to you, especially after you been so nice, but when we get inside, I got to handcuff you to a chair, or a bed, or somethin'." He frowned, remembering. "Only I ain't got no handcuffs, so it'll have to be a rope, if I can find any . . . . "

"To prevent my escape, I imagine." Carruthers sighed. "It's a shame, though. I really hate being immobilized in any fashion, you know. A minor

form of claustrophobia, you see; I even wear my clothing rather loose." He
thought a moment. "Suppose I were to give you my word of honor that I
would not attempt to get away?"

"Yeah," Harold said thoughtfully. "I guess that ought to fix it. Your word
ought to be good." He smiled, pleased with the solution. "You and me, we're
goin' to get along fine, pops . . . . . "

"Bloody idiot!" Briggs said, fuming. He and Simpson were riding the bus
into the city, their luggage on an empty seat before them. Simpson was fin-
gering the stub of his Corona-Corona, unwilling to light it and taste the fine
taste for what he knew would be the last time. Briggs raved on. "Maniac!
Imbecile! Going through our bags like that! And then making us undress — !"

"Tim — "

"And, especially, pouring out those bottles of brandy and champagne just
to make sure there was nothing else in them! We'll sue! Oh, we'll sue! We'll
make sure that Griddesby — "

"Griggsby. Tim — listen — "

"Whatever! We'll make him sorry he was ever born! And — "

"Tim, listen — " Simpson said sadly.

But Timothy Briggs, once started on a crusade, was not easily put off.
Fortunately, the two men were on the open upper deck of a two-decker, so
that the breeze carried away a good bit of the vituperation.

"And that Grimsby saying that the A.C. of Scotland Yard had given him
the tip himself! And then when he finally gets this Winterblast on the blower,
the man never heard of you or me or even of this Grumley! I wouldn't be surprised if he never even heard of Heathrow Airport! Oh, they haven't heard
the last of this, believe me!"

"Tim — "

"And get that long look off your face!" Briggs went on fiercely, studying
Simpson critically. "I said we'll sue and we will. We'll get back the cost of every
bottle, at today's market for the top brands, believe me! Plus damages. God
knows how many years went off my life when I watched that — that — whatever his name is — pour our brandy down the sink! We'll collect, don't worry,
every penny, so don't look so God-'elp-us! The world hasn't come to an end!"

"Tim," Simpson said dolefully, "for us, maybe it has." He held out the newspaper story folded to the story of their financial disaster. Simpson had held
the bad news back during their session with James J. Griggsby, feeling that
Briggs had enough to cope with at that moment without adding to his grief.
But Briggs could not be kept in the dark forever.

"What's this?" Briggs asked suspiciously, and took the paper. His eyes took
in the head of the story and then skipped quickly to the body. When he

finally looked up from the article, he did not — as Simpson had feared he might — try to take out his frustration by attempting to rip one of the bus seats out by its roots. Instead the usually pugnacious Briggs looked slightly dazed. "We're broke!"

"It looks that way," Simpson said sadly.

"No more brandy — "

"No."

"No more champagne — "

"No."

"Back to beer — "

"No. I mean, yes."

"Back to cucumber sandwiches — "

"Yes."

"Back to watercress salads — "

"Yes."

"No more Corona-Corona cigars for you — "

"Yes. I mean, no." Simpson contemplated the stub of his last Corona-Corona and then with a sigh tucked it back into his pocket. He tried to smile, to put the best face possible on it. "Still, we had a few good months of it, didn't we, Tim?"

"Blaggedy blam the bloggelly blodgedy few good months!" Briggs said brutally, and suddenly thought of something else. "Does Billy-Boy know, do you suppose?"

"He gave me the paper."

"Oh — "

The totality of the tragedy weighed so heavily upon them that it was only by accident that Simpson looked up in time to see they were almost at Swan's Park and their destination. He tapped Briggs on the shoulder and the two climbed down from the bus, carrying their bags, and made their way slowly to their club. Here they left their luggage in the care of the hall porter and walked into the lounge, expecting to see Carruthers, but their niche in the northeast corner was deserted, and from the lack of even a beer mug on the side table it was evident their friend had not yet made his appearance.

"Strange — " Simpson said, and frowned down at his shorter companion.

"Maybe he didn't feel like drinking beer," Briggs said bitterly. "Maybe he just went home."

"I'll just give him a buzz," Simpson said, and disappeared in the direction of the telephones. When he came back his long face was even longer. "His landlady said he hasn't shown up."

"Odd," Briggs said, and suddenly looked worried. "You don't suppose — ?"

"What?"

"Well," Briggs said slowly, "if Billy-Boy knows the bad news, who can tell how it might strike him? And you know the bus from the airport comes fairly close to the river in a few places — "

"No!" Simpson looked horrified at the suggestion. "Billy-Boy? Never! No," he said bravely, "something's come up, is all. We'll hear from him, you'll see. All we can do is wait," and he led the way to their alcove to begin the vigil with beer and biscuits and the remains of his last Corona-Corona. But they both knew the northeast corner of the lounge would seem awfully empty until Billy-Boy Carruthers once more joined them.

6

t the hour when Clifford Simpson was sadly lighting up the stub of his last good cigar, and when he and Briggs were sitting down disconsolately to their beer and biscuits, Billy-Boy Carruthers was also feeling a bit peckish. While it is true that in the course of his long and rather checkered career Billy-Boy had often been reduced to surviving on cucumber sandwiches and watercress salads, it was rare, indeed, when he had actually completely missed a meal of some sort. The only time he could remember occurred when he was returning from Great Mickle and the train stalled between Great Mickle and Little Modicum, with neither motive power nor dining facilities, for a matter of six hours. He had gone to Great Mickle to research his novel *The Mickle Monster Murders*, and while even its author only vaguely recalled the details of the plot, the foodless afternoon had never left his memory. At the moment he was beginning to remember it again.

"I say," he said to Harold, who had just returned from putting their guest's bag in the large bedroom adjoining the ample kitchen, "what does one do for sustenance in this establishment?"

"Huh?" Harold asked.

"Food," Carruthers said, elaborating. "Bread and butter, or even margarine; meat and potatoes; cabbages and kings without the kings. Things of that general nature."

"Oh!" Harold said, getting the picture. He waved an expansive hand around. "We got lots of food in the joint, and I ain't a bad cook, if I say so myself. Worked in the kitchen at Sing Sing and Joliet, and even at the big Q, and we got a lot better stuff than the garbage I had to work with in them joints."

"Excellent!" Carruthers said. "And exactly when do we eat?"

"Oh. I'll get some supper started as soon as Clare gets back. Don't worry, pops," Harold said reassuringly, "you won't starve here. Maybe it won't be no frogs' livers or whatever you rich guys are used to, but it won't be no poison, neither." An idea struck him; he was not completely insensitive to the social mores of his host country. "Say, pops, in the meantime, how's about I make you a nice cup of tea?"

Carruthers had been about to ask the large man to please stop calling him pops, when a more important thought interjected itself in his brain. He nodded at Harold pleasantly.

"Tea should do nicely with the sumptuous repast you undoubtedly will produce at the proper time," he said agreeably, "but what about something first?"

"First?" Harold was puzzled. Apparently there was something about the tea custom he had missed, because he thought all Englishmen drank tea first, last, and always. If they didn't, he wondered what Clare was going to do with all the tea he had bought.

"Something libatory," Carruthers explained patiently, "on the order of an apéritif. But not, of course, a cocktail. Something more manly, like brandy, for example, with champagne for a chaser."

Carruthers was beginning to see the advantages of being kidnaped. For a short while — or as long as he could possibly drag it out — there was no reason for him to return to beer and cucumber sandwiches. Time enough for that when the sad state of his exchequer became more common knowledge. It was too bad, of course, that Timothy Briggs and Clifford Simpson could not share equally in the beneficence, but as Harold Nishbagel undoubtedly would have put it, that was the way the ball crumbled.

"You mean — hard liquor?"

A terrible, frightening thought came to Carruthers. He swallowed. It occurred to him that upon entering the farmhouse he had seen no sideboard.

"This Clarence of yours," he asked, "is not an abstainer, is he? He does not, for political reasons, refuse to look upon the wine when it is red?"

Harold stared. "Huh?"

"I said, your Clarence does not remove his hat and stand at attention when the name of Volstead comes into the conversation? He is not a follower of Carry Nation and her crowd?"

"Naw! He's a Protestant."

"I mean," Carruthers said firmly, determined to get to the bottom of this most important matter, "is there liquid refreshment of an alcoholic nature in the house? Does this Clarence imbibe? Partake? To put it in a word — or three, to be exact — does he drink?"

"Oh!" Harold said, finally understanding. "Sure, Clare takes a drop now and then, though he ain't a lush by no means. You mean, is there hard stuff in the house? Sure, lots of it, and good stuff, too. I know, I ran bad stuff long ago." He looked uncomfortable. "Only Clare don't like for me to be drinkin' when he ain't around, especially when I'm supposed to be keepin' an eye on you."

"I see. Well, I certainly should not wish to go against the rules of the house," Carruthers said, vastly relieved that his first fear had been unfounded. "In that case, let me offer a solution. Why don't I have the brandy and champagne, and you have the tea?"

"Say! Yeah! That'd work!" Harold said, pleased that a practical answer to the problem had been found, and also pleased that his first opinion of the old man's brain power had been vindicated. Then he paused again, frowning. "But — is it good for you to be drinkin'? I mean, at your age? If somethin' was to happen to you, Clare would be sore. He'd be climbin' the walls — "

"If you mean that Clarence would be angry, which in your quaint way with words I suspect you do," Carruthers said, "may I hasten to add that if something unpleasant should happen to me, I should probably be equally perturbed, if not more so. However," he added philosophically, "at my age eating and drinking are about the only pleasures left. And the telly, I suppose." He considered that statement a moment. "On second thought, forget the telly." He looked around. "You do have a television set, I imagine?"

"Yeah," Harold said gloomily, "we got a TV in the other room, but Clare said to leave it off." He was at the cupboard over the sink; by opening one cupboard door a vast array of excitingly labeled bottles was revealed, and Harold was engaged in taking a few of them down.

"I begin to feel a kindred spirit with this Clarence," Billy-Boy said, and watched as Harold gingerly began to pour a few drops of brandy into a tiny glass. "Here," Carruthers said in a kindly fashion, "better let me do that. I've probably had more experience." He relieved Harold of the bottle and noted it to be of excellent quality. His opinion of Clarence rose. He replaced the tiny glass with a much more substantial one, poured himself a healthy dollop, took a small sip, nodded with appreciation, set the glass down and then wandered across the room. "And this, I gather, is the fridge?" Harold nodded. "With the ice?" Another nod. "And surely," Carruthers added, "your good cleaning woman will forgive me the loan of this bucket? There!"

He nestled the champagne bottle in ice in the bucket and settled down at the kitchen table, well pleased with his progress in injecting a more civilizing note into what had started out, at best, to be a rather graceless affair. He sipped his brandy, waiting for the champagne to cool, and watched Harold prepare his tea. When his large companion had finally managed the delicate task and came to join him at the table, Carruthers was feeling quite at home.

"I say," he said curiously, "what do your usual victims do to while away the hours until their ransom is paid — or is not paid, as the case may be?"

"We ain't got no usual victims. We ain't never kidnaped nobody before," Harold said, thus explaining his lack of knowledge on the subject. Then he paused, wishing to be factual with this kind-faced, fatherly figure. "Oh, yeah. I pick up a guy once when I'm workin' in Chicago, but we don't hold him for no ransom." He gave his imitation of a strangling beagle; for a moment Carruthers wondered in alarm if there had been something in the tea. He was about to come to his feet and pound Harold on the back when he realized it was just the large man's guffaw. "Only this character don't have time to get bored," Harold went on, his plastic grin in place, "because we drop him off the Clark Street bridge with a pair of concrete galoshes that same night."

Enough of this gibberish was understandable — for Carruthers had often frequented the foreign cinema in his more affluent youth — to make Billy-Boy suddenly reconsider the hominess of the ambient. When all was said and done, not only was the man across from him formidable in appearance but he had just admitted to a deed that the most sanguine could scarcely call a prank. Billy-Boy swallowed. Harold saw the swallow as well as the look that had crossed the elderly man's face. He hastened to reassure him.

"That was different, pops. That was completely different," he said earnestly. "This clown is practically committin' suicide. He's musclin' in on the boss's territory, not to mention makin' a play for Maisie, who is the boss's broad. You ain't done nothin' like that. All you done is come into some dough. And," he added, almost as if expecting praise, "we ain't goin' to ask for it all. Only half."

An old Euclidean — or Newtonian, he wasn't sure which — principle came back to Carruthers, stating that half of nothing is equal to nothing. He feared that with time and enough forehead-wrinkling, even Harold could come to understand that simple fact, while without a doubt this Clarence — apparently the brains of the outfit and from the quality of the brandy, a person of some perspicacity — would see the point at once. For the first time the thought of escape came to Billy-Boy Carruthers, but he put it aside sternly. Not only had he given his word, but escape to what? To beer and watercress salads? To glances of pity from a few at the club at their strangely reduced circumstances, and the gleeful sniggers from Potter and the others of his coterie? To the deadliness of lonely nights in his small rooms? For the time being, at least, he was doing much better than that.

And as to the future, what had Matthew said in the Bible? *Take therefore no thought for the morrow, for the morrow shall take thought for the things of itself.* Unfortunately, Matthew had not been content to leave well enough alone, but had to add; *Sufficient unto the day is the evil thereof.* He had been doing just fine, in Carruthers' opinion, until that word *evil;* and disposing of a kidnaping victim with or without concrete galoshes, to the most liberal interpreter, would definitely fall into that category.

And even had he not given his word, Billy-Boy had to admit sadly to himself that Clarence and Harold had selected well when they chose him over Tim or Cliff for their victim. The picture of him attempting to slip from a window — or even a large door — not to mention trying to outrun Harold, or even the absent Clarence, assuming him not to be on crutches, was enough to make him smile despite his predicament. The smile came as a great relief to Harold, who was already mentally kicking himself for ever having mentioned Chicago, let alone the Clark Street bridge.

"Like I told you, pops," he said earnestly, "you don't have a thing to worry about. Your pals will kick in and you'll be home in a couple of days. And as for what we can do to pass the time without the TV, we can talk, can't we? Clare, he don't like to talk to me much, I don't know why. And there ain't anyone else around here to talk to. That old bag that does the cleanin', she's more of a clam than Clare. That thing in the paper said you guys write books. Well, I could give you a couple of real plots, believe me! I could tell you a couple of stories that would turn your hair white — "

Carruthers held up his hand.

"Beyond the fact that my hair is already white," he said sadly, "I'm afraid my writing days are gone with Nineveh and Tyre — "

Harold frowned. "Who're they?"

"Not a song-and-dance team, although I admit they sound like it. Let me put it that my writing days are gone with narrow lapels and miniature golf, with trouser cuffs and neckties that light up, to bring it into your ken. Any stories you told me would be just so much waste. I haven't put a word on paper since 1925."

"And I wasn't even born then," Harold said reverently.

"If since," Carruthers remarked absently, and frowned. "No draughts in the house?"

"Naw," Harold said, rather surprised by the abrupt change in subject. "The place is built like a brick — I mean, they really knew how to build houses in them days."

44

"Draughts," Carruthers explained patiently. "What you Americans frivo-lously call checkers."

"Oh! Naw." Harold shook his head. "I ain't even seen checkers since one time in Dannemora."

"Or chess, then. Or backgammon," Carruthers said, getting desperate. "Or anything, if it comes to that. Even a deck of old cards and a worn bowler hat we could toss the cards into."

"No games," Harold said sadly. "And if we had cards we wouldn't have to throw them into no hat. We could play gin."

"Gin?"

"Sure. Gin rummy. It's a card game two guys can play. It's lots of fun."

Carruthers suddenly snapped his fingers. He honestly had forgotten.

"I say! By the oddest of coincidences, now that I remember, I just happen to have two decks of cards in my bag." He looked amazed, as well he should have, at his failure to recall the fact earlier; the cards had cost him enough trouble on the S.S. *Sunderland*. "They were mementos of a cruise we recently took on a ship called the S.S. *Sunderland*. With them — plus, of course, some forty-eight or forty-nine other decks, all the decks of cards the game-room steward had, as a matter of fact — I am pleased to say we were able to prepare for the game of Burmese solitaire. The preparation took us all night, with the three of us working like mad, Cliff and I on the cards and Tim running back and forth to the purser's sharpening pencils, but I'm happy to say the results were quite gratifying." His face fell at a certain memory. "Unfortunately, the captain — a stickler — requisi-tioned the sums we won for his own purposes — he said as evidence of some-thing or other, but one never knows. Possibly his salary was not as princely as his uniforms." Carruthers sighed bravely. "Still, I managed to salvage these two decks of cards as mementos of the affair, so I can't say it was a total loss."

"Gee!" Harold said admiringly. "You talk funny!"

"Yes," Carruthers said, acknowledging the compliment with a modest nod of his head. "Which," he added, "is precisely why I feel that mere conversation, despite the scintillation your remarkable efforts contribute, would be a rela-tively poor means of occupying time. Much better, in line with your latter sug-gestion, to play this whatever-the-name-of-it-is card game you mentioned."

"Gin rummy," Harold said, amazed that anyone in the civilized world had-n't heard of the game. Still, he supposed they probably didn't even have cards when the old man was young. He looked across the table. "You don't know how to play?"

"No," Carruthers admitted, "but I assume with your eloquence and com-mand of the language you will be able to acquaint me with the basic rules of the game in a mere matter of minutes." He added a trifle modestly, "In addi-tion to a flair for alliteration, I have a rather good card sense, you know."

45

"Well, all right," Harold said, and hesitated. "But I better warn you, pops, I'm pretty good at cards, all kinds of cards, and especially at gin. When I was workin' in Chicago, I had to play gin with the boss every night until he got sleepy or until Maisie come home from the club, whichever come first. And I had to see to it the son-of-a — I mean, I had to see to it he won every time. It ain't that easy losin' every game without givin' it away, pops, believe me!"

Carruthers looked at him curiously.

"And you believe your boss really cared whether you lost on purpose or not, just as long as you lost?"

"I never aimed to find out," Harold said honestly. He paused and frowned a bit diffidently. "Say, pops — you know, in this game of gin, sometimes guys, well, they sort of — well — bet . . . . "

"You mean, wager?"

"Yeah."

"You mean, they play for — money?"

"Well, yeah. It's sort of supposed to make the game more interestin'. I don't suppose — " He looked at the innocent features of his newly found friend and came to a sad conclusion. He sighed. "Naw. I guess not. You don't look the kind."

"One can always change," Carruthers said bravely. "One must always be prepared to learn."

"Yeah!" Harold said, brightening. "You're a real sport, pops. I won't make it too tough on you." He considered. "How's about a penny a point?"

"British or American?"

"Huh? Is there a difference?" Harold had never been able to understand the intricacies of the British currency system, nor had he ever faced the need to. Clarence handled all the financial matters in the household, nor would Clarence have had it any other way.

"There is a difference," Carruthers said sadly. "Not as great as it once was, or as it should be, but definitely a difference." He thought a moment and then nodded his head. "However, to eliminate this fiduciary confusion, why don't we simply forget the pennies, or pence, or whatever. Why don't we play, instead, for a few shillings a point?"

"What are shillings? They worth much?"

Carruthers sighed mightily.

"Again, not what they were, or should be. I remember a time — but I digress. To get back to shillings, why don't we utilize the decimal system for the purpose for which it was originally created and play for — say — ten shillings a point? In that way all we have to do is multiply the point difference in our score by ten and we'll know where we stand, what? Reduce the arithmetical difficulties, so to speak."

Harold had long since given up any attempt to understand every word Carruthers said, but there were still certain principles he wanted clearly understood.

"Yeah," he said doubtfully, "but the thing is, I don't want to see you get hurt, pops. Bein' nicked for the ransom's bad enough. So how much is that ten-whatevers in dough?"

Carruthers might not have heard him.

"And I'll keep the score so there is no confusion," he said in a kindly tone, "since the numbers are obviously strange to you." He reached into a pocket for a pencil.

"Sure, but how much — ?"

"The cards." Carruthers said gently, reminding his host. "In the top right-hand pocket of the bag, inside. It is not locked."

"Oh, yeah, sure," Harold said, and hurriedly arose to get the cards from his guest's luggage. Behind him Billy-Boy Carruthers decided the champagne was cold enough whether it was or not. He expertly removed the cork and poured himself a brimming glass, then added sufficient brandy to his other glass so as not to make his hosts appear parsimonious, after which he leaned back calmly, awaiting the return of Harold with the two decks of cards.

7

The matter of A.C. Winterblast and James J. Griggsby out of the way — for Clarence had been an interested observer of Briggs and Simpson being marched into custody — and having waited until he saw William Carruthers safely sandwiched into the car with Harold Nishbagel, Clarence W. Alexander now moved to the subsequent part of his program. Thorough in this as in every detail of one of his schemes, he picked a deserted telephone booth and called the *Daily Express*. Here he used the voice of a Disgruntled Subscriber, copying the accents he had heard on a television program dealing with the difficulties of life in the Midlands.

"'ere!" he said into the mouthpiece, once he had been connected to the Question-and-Answer editor. "What in 'er bloody 'ell is them three old men what won 'er bloody Jarvis award goin' to do with all 'er bloody money, eh?"

The calming voice at the other end refrained with an effort from asking in return what in 'er bloody 'ell business was it of 'is — the Q.-and-A. editor having originally come from Ormskirk himself — but instead remembered all the many lessons in proper language, as well as the demands of his position, and stated that the three elderly gentlemen referred to had only won a matter of twenty thousand pounds, which was not exactly the riches of Croesus in these inflationary days, especially when divided three ways, and that as far as the newspaper could discern, other than a small amount of this largesse that had gone for a few sundries, a trifle more for a cruise on the S.S. *Sunderland* and a very brief stay in Gibraltar, the balance had been wisely invested.

"Hummmph!" said the Disgruntled Subscriber — Clarence was getting quite expert on *Hummmph!* — and hung up. (Hummmph yourself, you bloody sod, said the Q.-and-A. editor, and slammed down the receiver.)

So the three old men had won twenty thousand pounds, and if he were to demand half, Clarence pondered, it would only amount to ten thousand pounds. Not a very great sum considering, as the calming voice of the Q.-and-A. man had said, the current inflation, and also considering that Clarence had at that moment — without Harold's knowledge, he hoped — almost three times that amount in dollars in a small safe he had installed at the farm, for Clarence never liked to be very far from his funds. He had often thought of what he might have gained had he had the foresight to sell the Bay Bridge instead, which was twice as long as the Golden Gate and therefore should have been worth twice as much, but he put the thought away as being both greedy and also, unfortunately, after the fact. Besides, he had been a stranger to San Francisco at the time, so he should be forgiven. Still, ten thousand pounds — roughly twenty thousand clams in real money — was, as Ring Lardner was wont to say, better than a poke in the eye with a sharp stick. And considering the small expenses involved, it could be considered practically pure profit.

He therefore stopped his speculation and put Step Three of his plan into operation by appearing at the nearest stationery store with proper gloves for the fall day, but inexplicably purchasing the cheapest paper and envelopes, both of which, the clerk was not averse to snidely pointing out, could be had equally at any ten-and-twenty-pence shop, particularly considering the modest quantity he bought. Not at all perturbed by the clerk's observations, and with a stamp obtained from an accommodating machine, Clarence next betook himself to a public convenience, where he locked himself into one of the narrow stalls, and using his briefcase for a writing desk, proceeded to draft the ransom note. He used printed characters, working laboriously but carefully with his left hand, and when he was finished he had to compliment himself on a job well done. He could not imagine anyone, facing the exigencies of that note, refusing to obey it. He folded the note neatly, tucked it into its envelope, and addressed it. He then sealed it and applied the stamp. With the ransom note tucked into an inner pocket, he then proceeded to tear up the rest of the writing paper and envelopes and flush them down the box. They disappeared with appropriate happy gurgling sounds, as if auguring well for the venture.

He emerged from the Gents feeling quite pleased with himself, and deposited the ransom note in the nearest pillar box, assuming an air as he did

49

so of a person — gloved — dropping a note — undoubtedly perfumed — to his loved one; he felt after all his planning and the success of the operation to that point, that he could permit himself this slight conceit. It was, in a way, a love note; but to himself, his greatest admirer.

This aspect of the job done, he took himself by foot to the proper railway station and had a gin-and-lime while waiting for the train that serviced, among other blighted areas, the village of Crumley-under-Chum. He was prepared to spend the evening reading, for Clarence never had ceased to try and improve himself, realizing the value of erudition — or at least pseudo-erudition, in the snagging of suckers. The old man, their paying guest, he was sure, after the adventure of his day would undoubtedly fall asleep as soon as he got some warm food in him; and it made little difference if Harold stayed awake or not after doing the dishes. It also made no difference if Harold spoke or not — as he had a tendency to do to excess — recounting tales of glory involving Chicago. Clarence had long since ceased to pay attention to the prattlings of his large confederate.

His train arrived at Crumley-under-Chum on time, and his taxi dropped him at the head of the lane leading to the farmhouse just as the sun dipped below the horizon, reflecting its great golden rays from the soft low-lying fleecy clouds, throwing lovely gossamer rose-tinted shadows. Unfortunately, the delicate shadows were wasted on the dank sedge, dismal rocks, rusty lawn-mower, and fetid ditch that comprised a good part of the visible landscape. But even this prospect could not reduce in the slightest Clarence's pleasure in his day. He unlocked the door and pushed into the house, locking the door behind him again. Through the intervening doorway he could see the two men seated at the kitchen table playing cards. So Harold was, in fact, entertaining their guest as per instructions, and while it was true their guest was not tied either hand nor foot nor even bound to the table leg with a sheet, at the same time there was no sign that he was making a fuss. With a smile at the ease with which things work out if properly planned, Clarence put aside his briefcase and walked into the kitchen.

Harold looked up with a slightly dazed expression on his face, as if he had not been expecting visitors and did not relish their appearance at the moment. Clarence smiled genially at both men, and then turned his attention to the fatter one.

"So you're the famous William Carruthers."

"I wouldn't exactly say famous," Billy-Boy said modestly. "Noted, possibly. Distinguished, if you must. Celebrated, if you insist. And you must be Clarence."

"Exactly." Clarence noted the bottles and the glasses, as well as the cold cup of tea at Harold's elbow. He nodded his approval. "I'm pleased to see that Hal has been taking good care of you," he said, and glanced at his confederate. "What about something to eat for our guest, Hal? And for us, as well?"

"In a second," Harold said briefly. "Soon's the game's over."

"Fine!" Clarence said expansively. Nothing could possibly spoil this lovely evening for him. He came to stand behind Harold, looking at his cards. "How are you doing?"

"Terrible!" Harold said tightly. "Awful! Pops, here, is luckier than a guy with two bicycles! I teach him the game maybe a couple hours ago, at the most, and already he schneids me six-across-Hollywood twice in a row!" He forced a smile. "Not that I'm complainin'; I ain't no sore loser. He plays good."

Clarence smiled indulgently and leaned over to consider the score pad before Carruthers.

"I can see," he said, amused by Harold's discomfort. "Eighty-four hundred points. Quite a few." His smile broadened. "What are you playing for? Matches?"

"Matches, nothin'! Ten somethin's," Harold said, and concentrated mightily on his hand for several moments before finally selecting a card and placing it on the discard pile.

"Shillings. Ten shillings a point," Carruthers said, explaining, and picked up Harold's discard. "Gin," he said brightly, and reached for the pencil.

Clarence gulped. *"Ten shillings a point?"* He reached. "Let me see that score pad!"

"Certainly," Carruthers said agreeably, "as soon as I score it," He counted the points in Harold's hand, totted up the additional points, and handed the paper across to Clarence. "That makes it ninety-four hundred and sixty points, I believe."

"At ten shillings a point!" Clarence still could not believe it. *"That's almost five thousand pounds!"*

"Is it?" Carruthers took back the paper and went into some complicated calculations along the border, licking the pencil point for accuracy. He looked up, beaming at Clarence in a congratulatory manner. "You're quite right, you know. I make it four thousand seven hundred and thirty quid, to be exact."

Clarence turned to Harold, his eyes narrowing, his jaw clenched. "And just how are you going to pay all this, dummy?"

"Pay it? How much is it?" Harold asked, wondering why Clarence was suddenly so unfriendly.

"Roughly ten grand! Ten thousand bucks, you idiot!"

"Ten thous — " Harold swallowed, looking dazed.

"That's what I said! Open your ears! Ten thousand dollars, lunkhead! And how do you expect to pay it?"

Harold was looking at Carruthers with wounded eyes.

"You should have explained how much we was playin' for, pops. I wasn't tryin' to take you. That wasn't very nice of you."

Billy-Boy Carruthers was quite willing to get into a discussion on the relative niceness of kidnaping as opposed to winning at cards, but before he could reply, his attention was drawn to Clarence, who had suddenly smitten himself on the brow. It had occurred to Clarence W. Alexander that he was almost as big an idiot as Harold, to be making such a fuss over nothing. The fat man was, after all, their prisoner, and while as a general rule Clarence normally honored gambling debts — although to be truthful he seldom faced them since he usually played with his own dice — in this case honoring a gambling debt was not even a part of the question, let alone the answer. If Harold, with his odd sense of fairness, got stuffy about it, he could simply add Harold's loss to their ransom demands and write them off. Or he could get the old man in a game of Parcheesi and win the money back. Not to mention the distinct possibility that, Harold or no Harold, they might well have to scrag the old man to keep him quiet after the ransom was paid, and it was a statistical fact that scragged old men never collected debts, gambling or otherwise.

All of this having flashed through Clarence's active and conniving brain in a matter of moments, he took a deep breath and smiled at Harold apologetically.

"I'm sorry, Hal," he said. "I shouldn't have lost my temper over a little thing like that."

"Sure," Harold said, instantly forgiving his friend. "Anyways, I can pay him out of my share of the ransom dough, Clare. It won't cost you a cent, my losin' like that."

"Of course. Of course," Clarence said in a conciliatory manner. "And now, how about a nice meal to finish off a nice day?"

"Sure," Harold said generously. "I got some beans and leftover veal I can make into a real *casserole Leavenworth*. Some guy shown me in Joliet. You guys wait in the other room. I'll carry in your drinks," he said to Carruthers, and shook his head in admiration for the old man, all previous irritation at having lost now dissipated.

Almost ten grand the old guy beat him out of, and him not even knowin' the game a couple hours ago, not to mention bein' six years older than God. Harold picked up the bucket and the brandy bottle in one huge hand, gathered in the half-filled glasses in the other, and carried them into the next room, setting them down beside Carruthers, who had settled himself in a comfortable arm chair. And that was another thing: the old man had put away enough hooch to knock even Maisie — and Maisie had been known to bend an elbow with the best — right on her full keister, and yet the old guy hadn't even got the slightest bit woozy. It just showed that gettin' old didn't mean the end of the world; and on that comforting thought Harold went back into the kitchen and began digging exploratorily into the fridge.

Leaving behind him in the other room an extremely thoughtful William Carruthers, no longer feeling quite as homey as before, and feeling far less of a kindred spirit with this Clarence just because the man had good taste in brandy and appreciated the artistic advantages of a turned-off television. Taking money from Harold with marked cards had simply been an entertainment; but the look in this Clarence's eyes when he apologized to Harold for losing his temper, was quite another matter. The thoughts that had engendered that apology, that had realized the total lack of need to pay that debt, had most certainly been of a lethal nature. And that was quite another matter, indeed . . . .

8

Despite the fact that neither rain nor sleet nor snow nor even dark of night, for that matter, were present to stay them — especially since it was eleven o'clock of a sunny September morning — the postal messengers of Her Majesty's Service still managed to make their appointed rounds, and in the course of doing so, dropped off a missive at the Mystery Authors Club addressed to Timothy Briggs and Clifford Simpson.

Potter, the secretary, frowned as he fingered it suspiciously. In all his years of tenure as secretary, the only other message he could recall any of the three receiving was when the Jarvis award had been given them some months before. He was also surprised to see the name of William Carruthers omitted from the cover of the letter, but this mystery, at least, was resolved for him when he made his way toward their niche in the northeast corner of the lounge. Since Carruthers was missing, and since the letter was addressed to the other two, it was obvious to Potter — who had several minor mystery novels to his credit himself, and who considered himself therefore quite a master of analysis — that the missive had to be from Carruthers, and nobody else.

And no wonder the old man stopped writing, Potter thought, taking pleasure from the concept, considering the awful state of his penmanship — or pencilmanship, rather. Printed, and barely legible, at that. Probably never heard of a typewriter, and wouldn't be able to solve its intricacies if he had! Must have driven his publisher crazy!

Satisfied with his analysis, and wondering how he might be able to work it into his next opus, he handed the letter over with a sniff and made his way back to his office, noting in passing that the old men had gone back to beer, and that Simpson was back to smoking those tarred bits of rope he used to smoke before. Probably wasted all that lovely Jarvis money, Potter thought with more than a touch of satisfaction, and then smiled as he could visualize himself making good sport of the fact with his coterie when they arrived for lunch.

"Silly ass!" Briggs said, making no attempt to lower his voice as he looked after the secretary with contempt, after which he brought his attention to the letter he had been handed. He turned it over to study it from all sides.

Simpson was leaning forward eagerly. "From Billy-Boy?"

"Not unless he broke his arm and was writing with his left hand," Briggs said, and then suddenly nodded, his writer's brain — or ex-writer's brain, that is — suddenly afire. Old habits die hard. "That's probably it. He's probably in some nursing home someplace with a broken arm. Probably couldn't stand the thought of cucumber sandwiches so he stepped in front of a lorry; it wasn't the river at all. Or maybe he's just faking the broken arm, just pretended to be struck by a lorry, to get the food they serve in nursing homes — although," he said, thinking about it, "that doesn't make much sense. But he was struck by a lorry on his way here to meet us, yesterday. He was carried to this nursing home, unconscious, and when he came to his senses he knew we would be worried, so he managed to get his hands on a pencil and some note paper, and — "

"How?" Simpson asked, intrigued.

"By getting a nurse's attention in the emergency area, of course — "

"How?" Simpson was nothing if not a perfectionist where plot was concerned.

"By — by — by pinching her — "

"Where?"

"In the rear. That's allowable these days," Briggs said with a snort. "We couldn't have gotten away with that in a million years; today it's almost obligatory. Anyway, once he had her attention, he reached over and took the pencil that was clipped to her uniform blouse just where her excessive cleavage started to become interesting. It's all the rage these days, that sort of stuff, you know," he said gloomily. "That's undoubtedly why we couldn't give our stuff away, even if we were writing. Which, of course, we are not."

"And the sheet of paper and the envelope?" Simpson asked, intrigued, still back at the nursing home.

"He simply asked her for a sheet of paper and an envelope and she handed them over," Briggs said shortly, no longer interested in the plot. "Plus a stamp, of course. They have scads of stamps in nursing homes."

"I'm sorry, Tim," Simpson said apologetically. Something had been tickling his memory and he finally recalled what it was. "But I already used that plot. Not the pinch in the rear or the excessive cleavage bit, of course, but the man pretending to be struck by a lorry just to be carried to a nursing home where he gets the attention of the head nurse and asks for writing material — "

"So you did!" Briggs said, also recalling the novel. "When he gets the pencil he stabs her to death with it, a pencil she had just sharpened herself at his request. I thought the symbolism was quite profound; for those days, that is, of course. You called the book *Up to the Eraser*, if I'm not mistaken."

"Exactly!" Simpson said, pleased that Briggs had remembered. "This nurse had jilted this man when they were mere youngsters in the village of Muggling-in-the-Fields, Berks, and now thirty years later he comes back from Borneo for his revenge. He had been raising garlic in Borneo, and had the habit of checking the tenderness of young garlic by poking it with a sharpened pencil, so when he went into this restaurant after the killing — "

"And they served him with garlic — "

"And he inadvertently poked it with the death weapon — "

"And the garlic turned red — "

"The waiter made a citizen's arrest!" Simpson beamed. Then his face fell. "*Up to the Eraser* never did as well as I had hoped for, now that I recall."

"A lack of appreciation by an unworthy public," Briggs said commiseratingly. "However, to get back to this," he said, weighing the letter thoughtfully in one of his little hands, "why on earth do you suppose Billy-Boy went to all the trouble of disguising his handwriting so successfully, when all he had to do was simply telephone us?"

"Possibly the nurse, while amply supplied with stamps, lacked the proper coin?"

"Possibly — "

"But, of course, one could open the letter and find out?"

Briggs nodded. "Not a bad idea." He slit the envelope with a thumbnail, removed the neatly folded sheet of paper within, and began to read it while Simpson waited anxiously. While the printing might not have given excessive pleasure to any Spencerian, it was quite legible. To Briggs it was also rather startling. "Well, well!" he said softly, his eyebrows rising dramatically, and handed the missive over to Simpson.

Simpson, mystified, put aside the tarred rope he had been nurturing, took the letter, and adjusted its distance from his aging eyes until he was able to focus properly. He read it quickly. "Oh, my!" he said, for the letter read:

Gentlemen:

Your friend, William Carruthers, has been kidnaped. At present he is still alive and in good condition. If you want him to stay that way, do what this letter tells you, and do it *exactly!*

Get ten thousand pounds together in small and *unmarked* bills and put them in an overnight bag. One of you bring this bag to Euston Station on September 15th — tomorrow night — which will give you plenty of time to cash in any stocks or bonds or get to a safety-deposit box to raise the dough.

You will take the train that leaves Euston Station at 11:16 bound for North Southerly. You will be in the last car. At approximately 11:58 the train is due to arrive at East Westerly, between Crumley-under-Chum and Glossop-in-Dorp. You will place the overnight bag with the money on the East Westerly platform and return at once to the train.

If there are any cops involved, or if our messenger who picks up the ransom money is interfered with *in any way*, your fat friend is *dead!* We kid you not!

There was, not surprisingly, no signature.

"Well," Briggs said, with an attempt to put the best face on a poor situation, "it's a good thing he didn't ask for one pound six shillings tuppence, instead of his ten thousand quid."

"Why?" Simpson asked, puzzled.

"Because I've got one pound six shillings tuppence," Briggs explained, "and after that I'd be flat."

"But what shall we do?" Simpson asked desperately. "This is dreadful! Shall we go to the police?"

"And receive one of Billy-Boy's ears in the next post with an added demand? No," Briggs said quietly, "that doesn't seem to be the answer." Faced with a real crisis, his normal belligerency had disappeared, replaced by a bit of hard thought. He tapped the missive thoughtfully with his forefinger as he studied it carefully. "Cheap paper, cheap envelope, manufactured by the millions, available at any stationers. Printed almost certainly by a right-handed person using his left hand — note the slope of the letters. Undoubtedly wearing gloves, and therefore leaving no fingerprints. By an American, incidentally, considering his language — "

"His language?"

"Of course. You will note that he says 'bills' instead of 'notes' and uses the word 'dough' for money. And he says 'cops' rather than 'police' or 'bobbies'. And that rather sophomoric 'I kid you not.'" Briggs shook his head. "But the

57

most obvious clue to his nationality, I should think, lies in the fact that he refers to Billy-Boy as being fat — "

"But Billy-Boy *is* fat," Simpson said. He had been following Briggs's masterful exposition with bated breath, but he could not help but interrupt in the interest of honesty.

"Of course he's fat!" Briggs said irritably, "but an Englishman would have been polite enough to say 'obese'!" He went back to the letter. "So, considering all I have said, the police will be utterly baffled, and since even being utterly baffled takes the police more time than our ransom note allows us, in the interim Billy-Boy could well be killed."

"I'm sorry I suggested the police. I wasn't thinking," Simpson said contritely, and attempted to rectify his error, but with only partial success. "I say, Tim," he said, coming up with something, "Billy-Boy had to be kidnaped by someone who was aware that we had money. Or, rather," he added unhappily, "who *thought* they knew that we had money."

"Which includes about everyone in the British Isles who can read," Briggs said sarcastically, "including, apparently, foreigners from our former colonies."

"True." Simpson was on the verge of wailing. He had never felt so helpless. "So what can we do?"

Briggs shrugged his small shoulders.

"Why," he said bravely, "we do the only thing we can do. Tomorrow night I shall be on the eleven-sixteen train from Euston Station for East Westerly, in the last car, with an overnight bag . . . . "

Clarence Wellington Alexander was a bit preoccupied. It had nothing to do with picking up the ransom money, for he had spent much time and thought in consideration of this problem and was sure he had covered all angles. He had selected East Westerly as the best place for the drop because as far as he could determine, nobody ever got off or on the train there, and he had come to the conclusion that the station existed only as an excuse to give employment to the ancient guard, without a doubt a relative of some Personage. In addition, Clarence had spent the past two hours inspecting the deserted platform from a vantage point across the road without sighting any minions of the law, before purchasing a ticket for Glossop-in-Dorp, one station up the line, and thereby gaining admission to the East Westerly platform. By now he was certain that no police were involved. But then he had scarcely expected the slightest difficulty when dealing with three ancient and helpless old men.

And he had his stub to leave the platform with the money when he picked it up; that afternoon he had come to East Westerly from Crumley-under-Chum, the next station down the line, with two passages in his pocket, and surrendered only the single stub, so he was also set in this regard. Reading English mystery stories had its advantages, although why the British Railways complicated their corporate lives with all these ticket stubs was a mystery in itself. Nor did Clarence expect the slightest recognition, or even examination, from the sleepy-eyed guard picking up the ticket stubs at the exit; the man looked as if he wouldn't notice the chorus line of *Oh, Calcutta* filing through *au naturel* with the band playing, even if he were wide awake.

No, picking up the ransom money was not the problem. Clarence's preoccupation came from wondering what to do with old mustard-suit Carruthers once the ransom was paid. Was it possible to put a big enough scare into the old coot to prevent him from going to the cops if he were freed? It was possible but far from certain; some of these crotchety old buzzards got up on their high horse once hard cash was taken from them. Possibly the threat that one of his dear friends would suffer if he opened his yap to the fuzz? But if old baggy-pants couldn't be sufficiently threatened when he was in their close custody, what threat would possibly bear fruit once he was tree?

Still, the question of leaving the old man's two hundred-odd pounds of lard buried in lye under the barn, or dropped down the well — which Clarence was convinced would get any future user of the well drunk for a week, considering the old man's capacity for booze — also posed problems. For one thing, there was no doubt Harold was becoming more and more enamored of the old buzzard. Certainly, Clarence thought with justifiable irritation, you would think that with the old man into Harold's pockets for more money than Harold even stood to gain from the caper, Harold would be head and shoulders in favor of scragging the old man, if only for sound financial reasons. But, oddly enough, such was not the case. For some inexplicable reason all Harold had was admiration for the old man. It seems the old coot had apparently once written a novel laid in Chicago, Harold's home town — although the old buzzard had never even been there — which had been titled *Petunias for Miss Blemish*, which happened to be one of the two or three books Harold had read in his life, and the only one he had actually enjoyed. In fact, Harold said he had never laughed so much at anything before or since.

Harold's loyalty to Clarence had never been in question up to now, but it was becoming more and more apparent that this singleness of heart was on the verge of being divided, and just how this would lead to Harold's co-operation in the elimination of old twinkle-toes, was hard to see. Clarence could, of course, also eliminate Harold, but this scenario was more easily written than produced. Harold had survived San Quentin, Sing Sing, Dannemora, Joliet, and the city of Chicago, and Clarence had a feeling he would probably survive Crumley-under-Chum. Besides, the truth was that Clarence had never killed anyone in his life, other than financially, and he would require Harold's

expertise for this chore. He also liked Harold in his own way; Harold gave
him someone to feel superior to.

His thoughts were interrupted by the sound of the approaching train, and
he put aside the aggravating problem of William Carruthers in favor of
reviewing his precautions in the matter of picking up the ransom, for while he
expected no trouble, it was in Clarence's nature to be prepared for anything.
Should the train come to a stop and uniformed figures come storming from it
wildly waving police batons and madly blowing whistles, Clarence would
assume his normal look of innocence and suggest that possibly they were
looking for the tall man with the reddish beard and the cast in his eye who
had just jumped from the platform and even now was legging it down the
road. And, he promised himself grimly, if that were the case, another letter
would go off tomorrow with a couple of old baggy-pants' fingers in it, after
which the fat man could practice shuffling cards with one hand!

But his precautions were unnecessary, his fears unfounded. The eleven
fifty-eight train for Glossop-in-Dorp and the other subsequent stations separating East Westerly from North Southerly and the end of the line, came
creeping into the station and took its place alongside the platform as if feeling its way in the dark, allowing its doors to be slid back in quite diffident
fashion, as if fearing the possible intrusion of passengers. Clarence stood
well back in the shadows, watching the doors of the last car. Sure enough,
someone was emerging there, coming to stand directly beneath an overhead
lamp that cast shadows over the scene. There was no doubt, despite the
shadows, that it was the short member of the triumvirate, Timothy Briggs,
and that he was, indeed, carrying an overnight bag. But instead of putting
the bag down and retreating to the waiting train as per instructions, Briggs
continued to stand there like a statue, his small hand gripping the overnight
bag tightly, until the train sighed electrically, tucked its doors reluctantly
back into their sockets, and slowly crept from the station as if its age made
the process painful.

From his position deep in the shadows, Clarence frowned. The action of
the small man was not in accordance with the demands of the ransom note.
Still, it occurred to Clarence — who was feeling a bit generous in view of the
fact that it was all working out without any unwanted interference from the
police or anyone else — that senile old men, faced with the necessity of deciphering a message written left-handed, and having to cope with a frightening,
mind-boggling problem at a moment's notice, could easily be forgiven one
small mistake. Let him who is without fault cast the first stone, Clarence
thought, recalling his early Bible training as well as a few times he, himself,
had loused up an easy deal. Besides, it was no insurmountable problem; all he
had to do was to relieve the tiny man of the loot in the overnight bag, direct

60

him politely to the east-bound platform, and see him on his way back to London, with a boot in the pants to help him, if necessary.

He waited a moment longer to make sure it really was not a trap of some sort, that the London bobbies had not come up with a midget cop in mufti in the manner of that astute Cleveland Indians manager who had brought a dwarf to the plate, and then called softly from his hiding place.

"Mr. Briggs!"

"Ah!" Briggs walked over, peering into the darkness. "There you are!" His eyebrows rose. "What are you hiding for?"

Clarence chose not to waste time in senseless conversation. "Did you bring the money?" he asked, and reached for the bag.

"Here! None of that! Not so fast," Briggs said testily, and pulled the bag back quickly. "Watch where you put your hands; that's how people get their arms broken! First I want to see Billy-Boy Carruthers and make sure he's in tip-top shape." He considered Clarence curiously. "You don't really think I'd hand over the bag to you without being sure of a thing like that, do you? Maybe your mother raised a brood of idiot children, but not mine!"

In the light cast obliquely from the overhead lamp, glistening in reflection from the spectacles covering Briggs's sharp eyes, Clarence W. Alexander saw that whatever else the old man was, he was certainly not senile. And while he was small, he also appeared feisty, and Clarence himself was no giant. He also was in no mood to start a wrestling match on a railway platform, deserted or not; he had no assurance that the guard inside, while undoubtedly sleepy, was also deaf.

"Just hand over the dough," he said, putting as much menace in his voice as he could muster, aiming for a tone somewhere between Karloff's Frankenstein monster, and Lugosi's Dracula. "Hand it over or your fat friend gets taken apart!"

Briggs, who had never seen either motion picture, looked at Clarence with pity.

"You could use a nasal spray," he said. "Anyway, we're wasting time." He started for the exit, paused, and then looked back with a frown. "Well? Are you coming, or not?"

Clarence gritted his teeth and followed. Somehow this was not the way he had visualized the scene. The two men handed their ticket stubs to the gaping guard and came out into the road. Briggs looked around.

"Where's your car? I assume you didn't walk, and you'd have to be pretty stupid to take a taxi for a ransom pickup — " He saw the car Clarence pointed to, and sniffed. "Not much of a car, if you want my opinion. I thought you Americans were up to a bit more in the way of swank. You mean you snatched Billy-Boy in this? Must have been a tight fit, is all I can say."

He climbed inside, holding the overnight bag tightly in his lap, and waited until Clarence had gotten in and started the engine. Clarence now saw the way things would have to go. Once they were on the road, away from even the few habitations East Westerly boasted, alone in the dark, he would simply pull off the road, take the overnight bag away from the little man, rap him on the skull a few times for luck, and dump him in a ditch. And then be off and running. It was a pity he couldn't take the time to gag the little buzzard, who certainly liked to talk, but everyone had to make sacrifices at times.

"And no rough stuff," Briggs advised, correctly reading Clarence's mind. "You don't look exactly like Harry Grebs to me, and I'm not quite as helpless as I look. You just do this my way, son, and we'll get along fine, understand?"

"I understand you've got a big mouth," Clarence said, stung, too irked by the little one's nerve to use any but his natural voice. "I also understand that I've got your fat friend, and if you want to see him in one piece — "

He suddenly stopped. Something else had just occurred to him. He now had his hand not only on William Carruthers, but also on Timothy Briggs. *Plus* the contents of the overnight bag. He saw now how foolish he had been to limit his demands to only half of the money the old men had won in the Jarvis award. Fortunately he had not told Harold exactly how much he was demanding, and with luck the subject need never arise. He glanced over at Briggs. So the little man wanted to do it his way, eh? Fine. In the morning another letter would go out, this time to Clifford Simpson, and the result would be the other ten thousand pounds the three had picked up. And if the three old coots had to go on the breadline afterward, that was a shame. We all have problems in this life. Play games with *him*, would they! Still, normal precautions would still be required.

"So you want to see your fat friend, do you?" he said. "In that case I'm going to have to stop and blindfold you, I'm afraid."

"You've good reason to be afraid," Briggs said tartly, and thrust out his chin. "Try it!"

"I don't think I'll need to try it," Clarence said with a faint smile. He reached over and before Briggs could bring up his hands to ward off the movement, Clarence had plucked Briggs's spectacles from his nose and tucked them into a pocket away from the little man. "That should do the trick nicely," he said with satisfaction, "especially at night." He smiled grimly and settled down to his driving.

At his side, Timothy Briggs, finally silent, sat and thought. Clarence's little game with the spectacles was meaningless; Tim Briggs had adopted plain-glass spectacles years before to give him a more distinguished look and partially compensate for his lack of height. Nor was it the fact that Clarence was smil-

ing like a cat that had gotten into the fridge; that smile was also easily interpreted. The kidnaper now had two victims in his hands rather than one. No,
the question was simply what would Cliff Simpson do when confronted with
another letter in a day or two?

Well, Briggs thought bravely, time enough to worry about that when the
flag goes down . . . .

9

At the time, admittedly many years past, when William Carruthers was busily engaged in putting to paper the adventures of Penelope Glottis and her ill-starred friend, Wilbur Tarbrush, in his opus *The Mickle Monster Murders*, and Clifford Simpson was similarly occupied tracing the careers of Cuthbert Sumatra, Bornean Garlic Raiser, and Hanna Hotspur, Registered Nurse, for his brainchild *Up to the Eraser*, Timothy Briggs was also working on a novel. This one concerned itself with the taking and holding for ransom of one Ming Toy Snodgrass by a certain Granville Graustark, Czar of Crime, and was titled *Bound and Gagged*. In the course of describing exactly *how* Ming Toy had been bound and gagged before being rescued from a dark, dank, filthy, rat-infested cellar by her fiancé, Herbert Marshgas, Tim Briggs had come to consider himself somewhat of an expert on the subject of kidnaping in general, and binding and gagging in particular.

He was, therefore, fully prepared to find Billy-Boy Carruthers bound and gagged in a dark, dank, filthy, rat-infested cellar, and one can therefore possibly forgive him his frown of disappointment upon being given back his glasses and ushered into the kitchen of the farmhouse, to find Billy-Boy not only ungagged and unfettered, but settled comfortably before the kitchen table, playing cards, with an almost empty brandy bottle beside his almost empty glass, and an almost empty bottle of champagne floating in a bucket more water than ice. It was as if Herbert Marshgas, coming to rescue Ming Toy Snodgrass, were to discover the young lady having cocktails with Granville Graustark, and enjoying them, too.

A Clifford Simpson would have taken that with equanimity; a William Carruthers with philosophic acceptance. But Timothy Briggs came from a different mold. He marched determinedly across the kitchen, lifted the almost empty brandy bottle, judging its contents, and then glared at Carruthers.

"You might have saved a little!"

Carruthers looked up in surprise.

"Oh, hello, Tim. What are you doing here? Have they kidnaped you, too? Well, well!" The other's complaint finally registered with him. He shrugged apologetically. "Regarding the brandy and the champagne — well, the early bird, you know . . . . " He suddenly remembered his manners. "I'm sorry. Tim, this is my good friend, Harold Nishbagel. Harold, this is an old acquaintance, Timothy Briggs."

"Pleased to meetcha," Harold said. "I seen your picture in the papers. But call me Hal, huh? I like it better." He grinned sheepishly. "Though I can't get pops, here, to call me anything but Harold."

Carruthers set down his cards.

"Harold," he said sternly, "one should never be ashamed of one's name, and particularly not with a fine name like Harold. Think of all the famous Harolds down through history: King Harold the First of England, who ruled from 1037 — if memory serves me — to 1040 — if I'm not mistaken. Then there was King Harold the Second — well, he only lasted a few months, so maybe we ought to forget him . . . . "

"Think of the Childe Harold," Briggs contributed. "Did Lord Byron consider for a minute calling him the Childe Claude, or the Childe Ralph? Of course not!"

"Exactly," Carruthers said. "Think of Harold Lloyd — "

"Think of Hark the Harold Angels Sing," Briggs said.

"Yeah," Harold said, conceding. "Well, all right, pops, you can call me Harold. But you!" He looked at Briggs severely. "You call me Hal, understand?" That dictum out of the way, he mellowed. "As for the hooch," he said generously, "there's plenty more where that come from."

"Excellent!" Briggs said, delighted. "Now, if you'll just point me in the general direction of the cupboard where you store your glasses, I'll — "

Clarence had been listening to this exchange in total disbelief. Now he had had enough.

65

"All right!" he said. "We're all through playing games, see? Hand over that bag, shorty!"

"Oh! Of course," Briggs said agreeably. He placed it on the table and turned, taking in its stead the glass Harold was offering. "That was very kind of you. I could have gotten it. And another one for what's left of the champagne before Billy-Boy hogs it all? In fact, you might even bring another bottle of the bubbly, with more ice, too, I think. And a reprise on the brandy would do nicely, as well, if you will?"

During all this conversation, Clarence had pushed aside the cards and opened the bag, upending it to dump its contents onto the table. The first thing to emerge was a pair of puce-colored underdrawers, seemingly suitable for a small elephant, followed by a few violently striped shirts, a couple of pairs of green-spotted socks, looking as if they were sprouting mold, and finally a pair of magenta-colored pajamas with moons and planets scattered generously about in various sickening colors.

("I dropped by your rooms," Briggs was saying to Carruthers. "I thought you might be able to use a change." "Thank you," Carruthers replied gratefully. "I *was* getting a bit dusty. All I had in my bag were soiled things from the trip, you know.")

Clarence was staring at the clothing on the table in shock. Now he finally brought his gaze from the cornucopia of color to the faces of the two. His jaw hardened; his eyes narrowed.

"All right," he said quietly in a cold voice. "I'm all through fooling around. Where's the money?"

"I told you before," Briggs said, trying to sound patient, "that until I had positive proof that Billy-Boy was all right, obviously there would be no payment." He shrugged, spreading his tiny hands. "Now that I can see he is quite well and in the best of hands, of course, as soon as I get back to town — "

Clarence sneered elaborately.

"A comic, eh?" he said. "All right, comic, make yourself at home while I go into the other room to write me another letter, this one a little stronger, or maybe in plainer English. And maybe I'll put one of your toes in it for luck, to show your pal Simpson that I'm all through playing games!"

"Why not one of my socks, instead?" Briggs asked hastily. Clarence had sounded all too deadly serious. "Or, better yet, one of Billy-Boy's socks? No surer means of identification has yet been devised than an article of Billy-Boy's clothing. Far better than toes, I assure you. After all, one toe looks pretty much like another — "

"Yeah," Harold said placatingly. "Anyways, we don't want no blood, Clare. I been havin' fun for the first time since we got here. Why don't you go write the letter? The skinny, tall guy'll come through with the dough, you'll see. I'm sure he wouldn't want nothin' to happen to pops, here."

Clarence looked at him. The omission of the name Briggs was significant, Clarence thought. He was sure Harold would not mind Briggs's being dismembered, but at the same time the chances were that this Simpson probably wouldn't mind, either. In fact, Clarence couldn't picture anyone who would give a package of used toothpicks for the big-mouthed runt. And for the time being, at least, it appeared that the fat man was under the personal protection of Harold. Well, Clarence thought angrily, that tall, skinny guy had *better* come through with the dough, because personal protection or not, someone was going to pay!

"*Grrraaagh!*" he said, unconsciously adding to his repertory of sounds one of the favorites of Timothy Briggs, and marched into the other room to compose his letter.

Harold looked up at Tim Briggs. "Hey! Do you play cards?"

"Why, no," Briggs said, and studied the familiar decks on the table. They were decks of cards which — together with many other decks — had given him and the others a hard night's work on the S.S. *Sunderland*. He looked up to see Carruthers' blue eyes considering him benignly. "No," Briggs said brightly, pulling up a chair, "but I'm always willing to learn . . . . "

In the interests of saving time, Clarence had the second ransom demand delivered by a messenger service. Clarence felt the risk was minimal and he did not wish to wait the extra day required by the post; he was wearying of his guests, and besides, the supplies at the farmhouse were being depleted at an alarming rate. Clarence had always thought that old people got along on a crust or two, but Carruthers ate enough for two — which might be understood, considering his size. What was difficult to conceive of was where Briggs put the food, for he ate enough for three. And both of the old men were amazing when it came to their capacity for brandy and champagne.

Simpson, sitting alone and disconsolate in the northeast niche of the club lounge, looked up hopefully as Potter made his way through the empty room with a letter. Potter, noting that now two of the three were missing, wondered just how he might work this into a book. Perhaps if he started with ten, and then had them disappear, or be killed, one by one until there were none — no, the critics would never accept it and it would be too complicated. With a sigh at the difficulties authors faced in concocting plots, he handed over the letter and started back to his office. Maybe if he started with five . . . .

Simpson could hardly wait for Potter to get beyond range before tearing open the letter. It read:

67

You, Simpson!

Now, listen you! Now the price is double, just for you clowns try-ing to be cute! Here's the last word! Twenty thousand pounds in an overnight bag on the platform of the East Westerly station at 11:58 tonight! We don't care how you raise the money, but raise it, or you'll be reading about your friends' bodies being dumped from a speeding car in tomorrow's papers!

Again, understandably, there was no signature, but this time, contrary to the last time, there had been no attempt to disguise the handwriting, and as a result Simpson was able to get the gist of the letter with less difficulty.

He pursed his lips and frowned. The tone of the letter, it seemed to him, was distinctly unfriendly, far more so than the first missive, and Simpson could only surmise that Tim Briggs had probably said or done something to irritate the writer. It would not be the first time Briggs had acted that way. And not only was the note, in his opinion, rather brusque — if not outright rude — but it also raised the ransom demand from ten to twenty thousand pounds. But certainly, if they had been unable to pay the ten thousand pounds, what on earth made the dear man think they could now come up with twenty thousand?

He read the note a second time, and frowned again. He could easily pic-ture Briggs's small body being dumped from a speeding car — although he hoped the kidnapers realized that speeding was illegal on many highways, not to mention dumping — but he doubted the kidnaper's ability to make good his threat in the case of the more corpulent Carruthers. Still, even one friendly body dumped from a car, even within the legal speed limit, and even where dumping was permitted, was obviously one too many. Besides, it was possible the man was merely using the dumping of bodies from speeding cars as hyperbole, when he actually had a much less dramatic plan for their dis-posal in his mind. Hyperbole, to demonstrate a point, and if not used to excess, was quite acceptable in writing, as Simpson well knew; he had used it frequently in those days when he was writing novels. He remembered well, in his book *Death by Dying*, where he had his villain, one Orville Smurch, in the process of tying the heiress to the railroad tracks, tell her that in minutes she would look like a plate of sautéed — Simpson brought himself back to earth with a start, ashamed of his mental lapse in view of the direness of his friends' predicament. This was certainly no time for daydreaming! Get on with it! Tackle the problem! Concentrate! Resolve!

But, how . . . ?

For one brief moment he considered seeking the help of the most intelli-gent person he knew, Sir Percival Pugh, but he put that thought out of mind almost instantly. If they couldn't pay the kidnaper, where on earth would they ever get the funds with which to pay Sir Percival, who was probably ten times more exigent than any kidnaper when it came to collecting fees? No, Simpson said sadly to himself, he supposed there was nothing for it except to go up to East Westerly himself, and try to explain the situation.

He fished in his pockets and came up with a few shillings and fewer pence. Scarcely enough for one-way fare, let alone a return. He thought a moment and then nodded. In his rooms he had the cardboard insert from a shirt that had recently come back from the laundry (and, he reminded himself, that was another bill that required payment! And people asking for twenty thousand quid just like that, as if money grew on trees! Although it would be pleasant if it did. Imagine a tree bearing one-pound notes! With his height he could easily beat any other four pickers, fill a basket while they were still trying to find a ladder . . .). With a start he brought himself back to the present. That cardboard insert was the same consistency, as he recalled, as the stuff from which they made train tickets. Now, if he could remember the size of a normal ticket, he could cut a duplicate out of that cardboard. A little crayon for the numbers and those inexplicable lines they put on railway tickets for no reason at all, and certainly at night, when most guards were sleepy, or preoccupied with wondering why their mates got all the good working hours, he should be able to pass it off as legitimate. He had used that ploy in a book once, as he recalled. Was it *The Mayfair Molester?* Or *Love on the Guillotine?*

He realized he was daydreaming again, and rose hurriedly to his feet. Then he sat down again. He had most of the day and half the night before he had to appear on the East Westerly platform, and he might as well spend most of those hours here. His rooms were on the way to Euston Station, and he was sure he knew exactly where he had that bit of crayon — in a shoe, he believed, or back of the clock — so what was the rush? It was in just such a rush, as he recalled, that his hero, Maxwell Valiant, nearly came to grief in his book *Tunnel of Hate.* Or was it *Three Fathoms High* . . . ?

10

Clarence W. Alexander, once again standing on the deserted platform of the East Westerly railroad station as the clock approached midnight — and beginning to feel like a native of the place — was a bit sorry, now that he had time to consider it, that he had demanded the full twenty thousand pounds from Clifford Simpson. Twenty thousand pounds, in his estimation, was a lot of money to pay for two old men whose main pursuits in life, apparently, were to eat and drink. Clarence knew, for example, that had he himself been the surviving member of the trio, he would no more pay twenty thousand pounds for the release of the other two than he would have gambled with someone else's dice. In fact, were he the surviving member, he would accept the kidnaping of the other two as an act of God, cash in as quickly as he could, and be on the next plane for distant parts, just in case either of the others survived.

On that basis he had a chilling feeling that Clifford Simpson would not appear, and that this trip of his to East Westerly had been unnecessary. That "one-for-all-and-all-for-one" malarkey was probably just so much newspaper talk; Simpson was undoubtably congratulating himself on his good fortune at the moment, and probably thanking his unknown benefactor — if he was anything like his two friends — with a glass in his hand.

In fact, Clarence had come so close to convincing himself he was wasting his time, that only the mournful hoot of the eleven fifty-eight, warning of its impending arrival, kept him from leaving the platform at once. But seeing the wavering lights of the train approaching, he decided to stick around for a few more moments, and he was therefore quite pleasantly surprised to see the tall cadaverous figure of Clifford Simpson actually emerge from the last door of the train with an overnight case in his hand. A moment later the case had been put down, but there the desired scenario ended; rather than retreat to the train, Simpson, like Briggs, remained standing beside the case, until once again the train, not yet thoroughly rested but aware of the demands of schedule, put its weary bones in motion and limped from the station.

Oh no! Clarence thought. Not again! With a sigh of resignation he came from the shadows.

"Mr. Simpson, I suppose?"

"That's 'Mr. Simpson, I presume,' I presume," Simpson said, and beamed down at the smaller man. "And speaking of presumptions, I gather you are the kidnaper?"

Clarence glared and looked around in the darkness. It was not the type of greeting he would have preferred, but fortunately the platform remained deserted, nor did it appear there were any persons within earshot, or even beyond earshot, if it came to that. He turned back to see that Simpson had picked up the overnight bag in the meanwhile and was waiting, a pleasant anticipatory smile on his somewhat horselike face.

"Now, you look here, skinny!" Clarence said grimly, with a feeling he had done the scene on stage many times before and would probably be condemned to repeat it endlessly until ticket sales weakened, or the theater burned down. "Why don't you just hand me that overnight bag and get on the next train to London? And go beddy-bye? And save us all a lot of trouble?"

"Oh, I really couldn't," Simpson said, sorry to have to disappoint this nice man. It seemed strange that such a pleasant-looking person should be a kidnaper, although Clifford Simpson would have been the first to admit he knew very little about the appearance of kidnapers. Villains who tied heiresses to railway tracks, now, they were a crew he had worked with extensively, but . . . He came down to earth, trying to remember what it was he had been saying. It finally came back. "I couldn't, you see," he said, anxious to explain his position, "not until I've seen Billy-Boy and Tim — "

"That again! Well, they're fine! But believe me they won't be fine for very long, if — "

"Oh, I'm sure they're fine, quite sure," Simpson said hurriedly, not wishing the man to think he would doubt his word. "It's just that I really don't know

71

how to handle the situation, and I need to ask their advice. Surely you can understand that, can't you?"

"No," Clarence said flatly.

"Oh, I'm sorry." Simpson shook his head in commiseration. "You have trouble understanding things, too, eh? I know how you must feel." He looked around rather vaguely. "Well, shall we go? The sooner I can discuss this with Billy-Boy and Tim — well, more Billy-Boy than Tim, because Tim seems to explode at times without too much advance notice. Or reason, either, you may have noticed — where was I?" He paused to think a moment and then beamed. "Oh yes. I was saying that the sooner I can discuss this with Billy-Boy, the sooner I'm sure we can resolve the entire matter. And that's what we all really want, isn't it? To resolve the entire matter?"

Clarence shook his head, a bit dazed by all the words.

"Now, look, you!" he said. "Just hand over that bag, see, and get yourself lost!"

He reached for the overnight bag, but Simpson resolutely held it above his head, coming close to some electrical wires there.

"Yes," Simpson said sadly, looking down at the other, "you *do* have the same trouble, don't you? Understanding, I mean. I'd repeat myself, but my experience is that it really doesn't serve much purpose. Much better to get on with seeing Billy-Boy and discussing it, believe me. So shall we go?"

Clarence came close to gnashing his teeth. Still, unless he tried to climb the old man like a telephone pole, there seemed little to do about it at the moment. Why, he asked himself desperately, had he made the basic blunder of arranging to meet these people on a railroad station platform, where a fuss could be heard by the guard? He should have set the meetings up in a dark alley, and come prepared with a lead pipe, except he would also have needed a ladder in order to strike this Simpson unconscious. He let his breath out slowly. Someone was going to pay for all the irritation he had suffered, he promised himself, one way or another! Probably Harold Nishbagel; the snatch had been his idea in the first place, after all.

"But you're going to be blindfolded," he said, adamant about this point. "Once we're in the car — "

"Oh no!" Simpson said pleadingly. "Take my word, I'd get the most dreadful headache. Besides, I assure you, I'm most inattentive. I have trouble getting from my rooms to the club. If it weren't for this kind old lady who owns the journal stand at the corner — "

Clarence sighed.

"Ah, the hell with it," he said hopelessly. "Let's go!"

Since gin rummy is basically a game best played by two, or by four if playing partners, Harold had decided that hearts was the proper game to accommodate the three of them, and at the moment he was pleased with the rapidity with which his two charges had caught onto the game. Here only fifteen or twenty hands had been played, and already each of them was into him for over a thousand pounds, and they were now only playing for five-somethings, rather than ten-somethings. However, with his share of the ransom money, he could not only pay off, he was sure, but even come out a few bucks profit ahead, and who could ask for anything more than that? Especially when he was having as much fun as Harold was having at the moment?

He looked at the trick on the table, disappointed but not surprised to find the queen of spades had been laid upon his ace of diamonds, since it seemed to happen with remarkable frequency. Maybe he could shoot the moon and get some of his dough back, except he seemed to remember that one or the other of his opponents had picked up a heart somewhere along the way. He was pondering his next play when he heard Clarence's key in the outer lock and looked up. Through the doorway from the kitchen to the living room, all three card players could see Clarence come in, ushering Clifford Simpson before him.

"Well, well!" Carruthers said softly, and turned to Harold. "Possibly some glasses for our friend?"

"Sure, pops," Harold said helpfully, and came to his feet at once, as Clifford Simpson came into the kitchen, ducking his head under the doorframe. Harold paused in his task and smiled delightedly at Carruthers. "Hey, pops! Maybe we can play bridge now!"

"Possibly," Carruthers conceded, and smiled up at his tall friend. "Clifford! Have a chair. Glasses will be here in a moment. To what do we owe this pleasure?"

"He got kidnaped like we did," Briggs said sardonically.

"Oh no!" Simpson said hurriedly. He did not wish his host, already apparently guilty of several kidnapings, to be accused of a crime of which he was innocent; that would have been eminently unfair. "Oh no! As a matter of fact" — he looked at his captor in embarrassment — "I'm sorry, I'm afraid I missed your name."

"He's called Clarence," Harold said, opening the cupboard and reaching for glasses. "I'm Hal."

"Thank you," Simpson said gratefully, and turned back to the others. "Well, as a matter of fact, Mr. Clarence didn't even want me to come along. He wanted to take my overnight case and wanted me to take the next train back to London. And go beddy-bye, I believe he said. No, it's my own fault I'm here, not his. I felt it vital that I discuss something of importance with Billy-Boy."

"And now that you *are* here," Clarence said wearily, "do you mind greatly telling us just what was so important that you wanted to talk to your fat friend about?"

Harold had come over with the extra glasses. Clifford Simpson smiled at him gratefully, sank into a chair, and poured himself a bit of brandy. He sipped it, raised his eyebrows in appreciation of its quality, took some champagne to follow it, wiped his lips and leaned back comfortably, at ease.

"I say!" he observed, looking about. "You don't have it half-bad here, do you?"

"Not half-bad at all," Briggs said, a rare admission for him. "Even the beds are fairly decent."

"And you will find Harold, in addition to being the most accommodating of card players, also to be an excellent chef," Carruthers added. "His *ragout-au-Dannemora* . . . " He kissed his fingers to indicate the merit of Harold's cuisine.

"And I don't think they ever heard of cucumber sandwiches in the States," Briggs added, "or at least not in the places where Harold learned to cook. I've only been here a day, it's true, but if they even have watercress in the house, I haven't seen it — "

Clarence slammed his hand on the table, bringing silence.

"All right, you clowns," he said, his voice tight. "Let's get on with it!" He turned to Simpson. "Talk! Just what was it you wanted to discuss with old baggy-pants, here?"

"Why," Simpson said, as if surprised he hadn't mentioned it before, "the fact that we have no money, of course — "

There was sudden silence.

Clarence stared in shock. Harold watched breathlessly, as close to high drama as he could ever remember. Carruthers leaned back in his chair, idly inspecting the ceiling. Briggs frowned and made a face.

"Cliff," he said querulously, "was it absolutely necessary to offer that completely unsolicited information? Especially at this particular time? Couldn't you have waited awhile? A few days, or even better, a few weeks? Now we'll probably get kicked out of here." He sighed and reached for the brandy, as if to be sure to have at least one more drink before being evicted into the unfriendly night.

"Well, I really didn't know what to do or what to say," Simpson said unhappily. "That's what I wanted to talk to Billy-Boy about, to ask him precisely what to do or what to say under the circumstances. I'm awfully sorry if I — "

"It's probably as much my fault as yours, Cliff," Carruthers said in a conciliatory tone, bringing his eyes down from the ceiling. "I suppose I should have insisted upon waiting until we could discuss the matter among ourselves in private — "

Clarence came out of his daze. His hand bounced off the table once again, scattering cards.

"Wait a second! Wait a second!" he said harshly. "What do you mean, you have no dough?" He reached over and grabbed the bag Simpson had brought, opening it roughly, upending it, shaking it furiously. Two pair of worn socks fell out, and a frayed handkerchief followed by a dog-eared cheap edition that Simpson had been reading on the train. Clarence stared at this detritus.

"I'm afraid it's the truth," Carruthers said regretfully. "Believe me, we feel as badly about it as you." He looked at the bottles of brandy and champagne as a French prisoner might look back at his sweetheart on the docks of Marseilles as he was being carted off to Devil's Island, never to return. "It is a sad fact but true. As you Americans are wont to say — if one can believe the cinema — the three of us are cracked."

"That's broken," Briggs said critically.

"You mean, broke," Harold said, pleased to be able to help.

"Shut up! Shut up! All of you!" Clarence glared from one to the other, ending with Carruthers. "What do you mean, broke? What about that award you guys won? That Jarvis whatever? Was it phony?"

"No, it was quite legitimate. Twenty thousand pounds," Carruthers said, and sighed deeply at the memory. "Twenty thousand of the best. We spent a quid or two for new suits, we admit, and a trifle here plus a trifle there. And we took that cruise on the *Sunderland*, you know, plus those few days in Gibraltar — "

"Peanuts!" Clarence snarled. "What about the rest? The paper said you'd invested it!"

Carruthers nodded. "And so we did. Poorly, I might add. So that now it is gone." He intoned the words tragically and spread his hands. "Gone, like chaff before the winds — "

"Like free ices at an orphans' picnic," Simpson contributed dolefully.

"Like Safe-Cracker Sam before the uniformed minions of the law, once they had him in their ken," Briggs came up with, and defended his selection. "That was from my book — "

"Shut up! Shut up!" Clarence glared murderously. "Forget *how* it went. *Where* did it go?"

"To that big bottomless safe in the sky to which all poor investors donate," Carruthers said sadly.

"To 'the undiscover'd country, from whose bourn no traveller returns,'" Simpson said, and despite the tragedy of the loss he could not help beaming, albeit a trifle lugubriously. "I remembered! I remembered! *Hamlet*, Act three, Scene one!"

"To that — " Briggs hesitated and then gave up.

"Shut up! Shut up!" Clarence sounded distraught.

Carruthers sighed deeply.

75

"My dear sir," he said commiseratingly, "believe me when I repeat that we feel as badly about the situation as you. Harold informed me you only wished half of our capital; we have lost it all. But it is truly gone. Gone, as Clifford just mentioned, to that undiscovered something from whose something else no somebody else ever returns. Take my word for it, sir. We are, indeed, impecunious, impoverished, destitute, moneyless, or pauperized, whichever you prefer."

Clarence fell into a chair, stunned.

"But people don't kidnap people who don't have money," he found himself saying.

"As a general rule, I believe that is probably correct," Carruthers said, agreeing. "There are, however, exceptions, and I'm afraid this is one of them."

"You honestly mean you can't pay a ransom? Of any size? Not even a little one?" Clarence was trying to comprehend the dismal fact, to clutch at straws. "What about your friends?"

"My dear man," Carruthers said, truly saddened by the other's lack of understanding, "if we didn't have many friends when we were in possession of these funds — and the slightest research on your part will indicate that we didn't — how many friends do you think we have now that we are penniless?" He paused a moment, thinking, and then frowned. "Did I leave that one out before? No matter. The fact is, without money people are usually without friends."

It was all too true and nobody knew it better than Clarence. Nor did he doubt for a moment that the old men were telling the truth. In the first place, he was sure that with money they would have paid the first ransom demand without hesitation and he would have been rid of the entire bunch days before. In the second place, he was sure the innocence in those china-blue eyes would never permit their owner to bandy the truth. And lastly, of course, with idiots like these three, it must have been duck soup for some sharpie to sell them worthless stocks. He just wished he had gotten to them first.

Harold had been listening in silence, his brain struggling with the attempt to translate all the words flowing in to him from all directions into meaningful pictures his mind could study. It seemed to him that if he understood the conversation correctly, the old men were saying they had lost all their moola and were flat busted. But something occurred to Harold, burrowing itself through his subconscious to titillate the proper nerve ends and generate itself into verbal expression.

"Hey!" he said suddenly. "You guys ain't broke!"

"We're not?" Carruthers asked, surprised.

"We're not?" Briggs asked, sarcastically.

"We're not?" Simpson asked, doubtful but wishing to be convinced.

"Not you, skinny," Harold said disdainfully, dismissing the thin man. "I ain't even played with you, not yet, anyways. I mean them two. I owe them dough. I owe pops a bundle, and I even owe shorty, here, a little bit."

"Roughly a thousand quid," Briggs said, "if you call that a little bit."

"Whatever." Harold frowned as a second thought wriggled its way past the bone, interposing itself on the first. His face fell. "The only thing is, I was goin' to pay you guys out of my share of the ransom dough. Now I guess I'll just have to owe it to you."

"As someone once remarked," Carruthers said, "that is supposedly better than cheating us out of it. Although," he added, "that never quite rang true, to me."

Clarence had been listening to this exchange without paying too much attention to it. He was trying to console himself that not all capers worked out one hundred per cent, and also that he hadn't really needed the money; but the fact was that Clarence was unhappy. He hated failure. Not only was he to gain nothing from his efforts — and his detailed planning and execution on such short notice deserved better than that — but he was also out a goodly sum from the amounts of food and liquor that had been consumed by his guests, for at heart Clarence was a miser. His *non-paying* guests, he reminded himself bitterly. He could still, of course, take out his feelings of frustration by dropping the three of them down the well, although he was fairly sure the tall one's head would remain well above the water line when he was through. And burying them under the barn would entail too much excavation to dispose of the fat one, plus the fact that the tall one's feet would probably stick out. They really didn't build barns in England like they did in Wapakeneta, he thought bitterly.

But there was really no purpose in getting rid of the three old men, now. Not from life, that was, though certainly from the farm. And particularly from his larder.

"Tomorrow!" he said coldly, and jerked his thumb authoritatively in the direction of the door and, symbolically, all of the wide world beyond. "Out! Tomorrow, all of you freeloaders — out!" He did not appreciate it, of course, but had he been ejecting Eliza into the snow, baby and all, he could not have done the voice better.

"Aw, gee," Harold said plaintively. "Can't they stay another week or so? We still got lots of grub and it'll be lonely after they're gone. And I oughtta get a chance to win back some of my dough. We was goin' to play bridge, see, now we got four hands, and when I was in the big Q, me and this guy in the next cell — a killer from Spokane — we was the cellblock champions — "

"Keep quiet, Hal." Clarence looked at the three. "Tomorrow!"

"Wait a moment," Briggs said in an unusually placating tone for him. "If you can't see your way clear to our remaining another week, how about five days?"

"Or even three?" Simpson suggested.

"I know!" Carruthers said, snapping his fingers as he solved the dilemma. "Why don't we simply compromise on four? It's a nice round — or, rather, square — number."

"So is six," Briggs pointed out.

"Or eight. Or ten — " That was Simpson in the interests of accuracy.

"Tomorrow!" Clarence said direly, and came to his feet. His tone indicated all too clearly he was through playing potsie. "The three of you deadbeats — tomorrow! Out!"

11

The three old men sat around the kitchen table and alternated between looking at each other disconsolately and staring at the cupboard even more disconsolately, for before Clarence and Harold had gone off to bed, Clarence had locked the cupboard and with it the brandy and champagne. ("Drink water!" he had said cruelly before going to his rest. "It's good for you!")

"Good for us!" Briggs said, and made a face. There was silence for several moments, then — "I wonder," Briggs said in a more thoughtful tone. The other two looked at him questioningly. "Well, I mean," he went on a bit querulously, "can he do that to us? Kick us out into the night, so to speak? After all, he kidnaped us, or anyway you and me, Billy-Boy. That gives him some degree of responsibility, don't you think?"

"You mean like the Chinese?" Simpson said. "If you save a man's life, you're responsible for him. But," he added, thinking about it, "this Clarence didn't really save our lives, did he?"

"For a few meals he did, or rather Harold did," Briggs maintained.

Carruthers considered the idea and shook his head regretfully. "I rather doubt it would stand up in court. A good barrister would put holes in it in a minute."

They fell into silence. Then Briggs seemed to perk up again.

"Or maybe we ought to go the other way. Threaten to report him to the authorities for holding us against our will. That's definitely against the law, and it'll give him pause, at least; make him think. It ought to gain us a few more days here," he said, in an optimistic tone that did not truly reflect his feelings, "and by then maybe we can think up something else."

"No," Carruthers said sadly. "He certainly isn't holding us against our will at the moment. Nor did he ever actually hold us against our will. Certainly not me."

"But if he *thought* he did — " Simpson said hopefully.

"No. Clarence is far too smart for a mistake of that nature. Nor would any policeman in the world buy it. Holding people against their will by feeding them brandy and champagne? And Harold's *coq au Quentin?*" Carruthers sighed and shook his head.

"How about the money Harold owes us?" Briggs said, never one to give up easily. "I know he doesn't have it, but he could go out and rob a greengrocer or someone, couldn't he? It's a legitimate debt, after all . . . . . "

"A legitimate debt? Playing with marked cards? Stop it, Tim," Carruthers said sternly. "No, we must take our medicine like little men. It's over, but let's try to look at the bright side. It was a short reprieve from pauperhood, it's true, but it was a reprieve, none the less."

"Great!" Briggs said in disgust. "You had three whole days of it; I only had one."

"I came a bit late, didn't I?" Simpson said. There was no envy in his voice, for envy did not exist as a Simpsonian sin; there was merely recognition that for some unknown reason God had arranged it so when it was raining soup, the Clifford Simpsons of the world would be out there in the street with forks. "Still," he added, thinking back on it, "I did manage one drink, didn't I?"

It was a rhetorical question and one nobody chose to answer.

"What I want to know," Briggs said in a small voice, his anger suddenly drained from him, "is what do we do now? Go back to starving in a gentlemanly manner?"

That question also seemed to require no answer, or if it did, it was an answer none of them could think of. They sat in dejected silence until Billy-Boy Carruthers heaved himself to his feet. He tried to smile bravely at the others.

"What was it Sir Percival always used to say?" he asked. "Faith and patience, patience and faith. That's what we require. Something will turn up, I'm sure."

"Our toes, most likely," Briggs said glumly.

"Quite," Simpson said, agreeing sadly. He glanced at the kitchen cupboard once again. "If only we could get into that without making too much noise — "

"No way," Briggs said positively. "I've been looking at it. It's built to last. And that Clarence is probably the snide type to be a light sleeper."

"But if we *could*," Simpson said hopefully, "at least we would be able to leave here with a few bottles to help us through the first few days at the club . . . . "

"My advice," Briggs said cruelly, "is not to think about it."

"I suppose not," Simpson said, and suppressed a yawn. He came to his feet. "I'm off to my rest," he said. "At least when I'm sleeping I'm not thinking of food or drink."

"I agree," Carruthers said, and turned toward the bedroom. "Coming, Tim?"

"No," Briggs said dourly. "I'm in no mood for sleep. I think I'll read a bit, first."

"As you will. Well, ta — "

"Ta," Briggs said dispiritedly, and got up to move into the library.

When Josephus Avery the First first brought his bride across the threshold of the Avery farm back in the year 1748, she made him promise that while they both knew he was an uneducated son of the soil and condemned by his economic position to remain so, there was no reason why any son of his should also so remain. And to further this worthy purpose, Mrs. Avery began to buy books as soon as she felt the stirring within her that was eventually to become Josephus Avery the Second. Josephus, Junior, ended up getting the education his father had been denied, graduating in due course with honors from Oxford with a degree as an Itinerant Egyptologist, the first but certainly not the last of the Avery clan to go onward and upward in the field of higher learning.

And, as the Averys continued to beget generation after generation and continued to worship the golden calf of education, each ensuing one added to the library, until at the time of which we speak, the Avery collection of tomes had become, if not impressive in quality, at least large. The farm, of course, had continued to suffer from the mismanagement those with higher degrees from University tend to display toward granges, and although Josephus Avery the Ninth attempted to stay this decline by studying animal husbandry at both Eton and Cambridge, the fact was that by the time he took his honors the last of the farm animals had starved to death, and the land was being whittled away for taxes. The result, coming many years later as these things often do, was that in the year 1921 Josephus Avery the Twelfth had been forced to put the farmhouse itself up for hire to who would have it, and it had remained rental property for all the many years since.

But the library had never been sacrificed and remained one of the outstanding examples of literary mishmash in a country where libraries of confused collections are far from unknown, for the Averys, like other Englishmen dedicated to books, were of various shades of literary taste. And it was for this reason that Timothy Briggs, studying the shelves in search of something that might induce slumber, or at least bring on the degree of lethargy necessary to allow him to forget his sea of troubles, was both surprised and pleased to see one of his own epics, written lo! these many years before, among the jumble of titles that faced him above his head from the library walls.

He stared at the book almost reverently for several moments before pulling up a stool to climb up and take the book down, but as he did so he appeared to disturb something behind the volume, because there was a brief movement of some sort and then some object detached itself from its alcove in the gloom behind the Briggs opus, and tumbled to the floor. With a frown Briggs climbed down from his stool, put aside his own book, bent, and picked up the object, bringing it closer to the light.

It was a rolled-up bit of material Briggs guessed was parchment from the rather boardy feel of it — he had once had a pair of kid shoes that had also gotten stiff, although from rain, not age — tied about with a faded and brittle ribbon, and covered with the dust of generations. In a sudden wonder that he might have inadvertently stumbled upon something valuable, Briggs took a deep breath, blew the dust away, sneezed violently several times as a result, and then carefully untied the ribbon, laying it aside. He unrolled the parchment gingerly, and found himself facing this:

PRAESES ET CURATORES UNIVERSITATIS
CANTABRIGIAE OMNIBUS AD QUOS HAE LITTERAE PER-
VENERINT SALUTEM
J. AVERY IX
PRO MERITIS EIUS AD GRADUM LITTERARUM DOCTORIS IN
CULTORE
SUIS ADMISIMUS EIQUE DEDIMUS ET CONCESSIMUS
INSIGNIA
ET JURA OMNIA AD HUNC GRADUM PERTINENTIA DIE XIV
MENSIS JUNI ANNO DOMINI MDCCCVC

When Timothy Briggs had gone to school in Newcastle-on-Tyne as a child, Latin was among the dozen or so studies not offered to the children of miners, but he had seen enough of the stuff in hymn books and on doctor's walls at least to recognize it for what it was. He frowned. Clifford Simpson, he knew, and William Carruthers, he suspected, had had classical educations, and it was but the work of a moment to reroll the scroll, tuck the ribbon carefully into his pocket, and make his way to the bedroom.

Although both Carruthers and Simpson were in their respective beds, neither was sleeping. Billy-Boy, decked out in the horoscopic nightmare Briggs had brought him for pajamas, was lying atop his bed looking like an advertisement for a color-blind fortuneteller. Simpson in his long underwear, looking like a cotton-covered carpenter's rule folded at the knees, was lying on his back staring at the ceiling. Briggs got right to the point.

"Cliff," he said, "do you read Latin?"

"Of course," Simpson said, surprised. "Doesn't everyone?"

"I don't, for one," Briggs said shortly, and unrolled the scroll, holding it out. "What do you make of this? It looks older than God. Has it any value?"

"Let me see — " Simpson draped himself over the edge of the bed and took the parchment from Briggs, while Carruthers got up on one elbow to watch interestedly. Simpson held the parchment flat beneath the lamp while he studied it. "Well," he said at last, "it goes on and on, as these things usually do — one would think they were paid by the word — but what it's trying to say is simply that a certain J. Avery the Ninth, whoever he might be, completed all the studies necessary to obtain a degree from Cambridge in the field of pig-farming, on a date in June of the year 1895." He frowned. "I didn't even know they taught pig-farming at Cambridge. Oxford, yes, but Cambridge — ?" He looked up. "At any rate, is that what you wanted to know?"

"A diploma! A bloody diploma!" Briggs said in disgust. "For a bloody pig-farmer, yet! And I thought I might have stumbled on something that could put a quid or two in the bank for us!"

"I'm sorry," Simpson said contritely.

"That's all right," Briggs said, trying to sound magnanimous, but finding it difficult to hide his disappointment. "I suppose it really wasn't your fault." He took a deep breath and shrugged. "Ah, well, back to the library again. Believe it or not, I found a copy of one of my old books on the shelves there. It's called *Mayhem on Monday*, if any of you recall it. I think I'll read it again, and see how smart I was in those distant days."

"Hold it!" Carruthers said suddenly, and sat up, swinging his legs over the edge of the bed.

"Why hold it?" Briggs asked curiously. "I don't believe it was all that bad a book. It's about this Irish washerwoman, you see, who was found drowned in one of her tubs — the rinse one, as I recall. It seems — "

"No, no!" Carruthers said impatiently. He was in the process of ridding himself of the pajamas. He drew his shirt on over the money belt, pulled on his trousers, and tucked himself in. "That parchment — that diploma. May I see it?"

"Of course," Simpson said, mystified by Billy-Boy's attitude, and handed it over. Carruthers paused in the task of buttoning up, allowing his trousers to slide to the floor as he took the old scroll and unrolled it, holding it apart as he studied it. He considered the face of the scroll for several moments and then turned the parchment over, studying the back. The presence of a few small lines, tiny cracks occasioned by the age of the ancient document, seemed, for some unknown reason, to please him inordinately. He smiled broadly and put the parchment down long enough to allow him to complete his buttoning and suspendering, after which he returned to the scroll, studying it intently.

"What's the matter?" Briggs asked curiously. "D'you think it's a fake or something? Do you suspect this J. Avery the Ninth never got his degree in slopping pigs?" He suddenly snapped his small fingers, his tiny eyes alight, the ex-writer in him coming to the surface. "That's it! There's an idea! The truth is that Josephus Avery the Ninth was on the verge of failing his thesis in sow-scrubbing, or wart-hog wallowing, or piglet-priming, or whatever made up his final examinations, and he knew if he came home without his diploma, his father — " He paused for the briefest of moments to reconsider. "No, make that the buxom daughter of the wealthy pig-farmer next door — would never allow him to hold hands with her again — "

"Which would have broken his heart, since she owned a Poland China sow and he had a Tamworth boar, and he had always dreamed of a double ceremony," Simpson went on, taking up the story, his imagination charging along at top speed, "so he went to this local forger for a false diploma, and luckily for him the man happened to be a Latin forger, since all the forges in the neighborhood had originally come from Milano, in Italy. And when — "

"Quiet, you two!" Carruthers said sharply. "Beyond demonstrating why we can no longer get published — and raising the question of how we ever did in the first place — this matter happens to be serious!"

"Of course it's serious," Briggs said, his tiny eyes twinkling. "Look at the condition of this farm! It's simply disgraceful. But if J. Avery the Ninth can marry the rich girl next door, it will not only handle the matter of the overdue mortgage payment, but it will start a new dynasty, and we all know how dynasty books sell!"

"Like nappies at a seaside creche," Simpson said, inspired.

"Like peanuts at a children's zoo," Briggs said.

"Like ale at a busman's picnic," Simpson offered.

"Like spaghetti at a convention of nearsighted sparrows — "

"Like — "

"Quiet!" Carruthers cut in sharply, frowning. "I'm trying to think!"

"What's the matter?" Briggs asked curiously, suddenly sober. "Do you think it might have some value after all?"

"Do you consider a few bottles of brandy and the same of champagne to have value?" Carruthers demanded.

"We do!" It came as a chorus.

"Then this scroll might indeed have value," Carruthers said, and smiled enigmatically. "Tim, does this vaunted library where you happened to unearth this relic, happen to also boast so mundane a volume as an encyclopedia?"

"It must have," Briggs said, mystified. "It had about everything else. Why?"

"Because I'm beginning to get an idea," Carruthers said, "and about time, too." He shook his head in disgust. "Imagine! Kidnaped by a rank amateur, and then made to endure the ultimate in ignominy — being booted out into the cold — !"

"It really isn't all that cold," Simpson said, thinking about it. "When I left London, the temperature — "

"Cliff!" Simpson fell silent. "Suffice it to say the situation is not to be tolerated. Cliff, get dressed. Get your bag packed. Tim, you do the same. I'll just throw these things of mine into my bag — " He did just that and fastened the latch. "There! Now, let's all go into the library. Might as well take our bags with us — "

"We're leaving?" Briggs asked, astounded. "Of our own free will?"

"You're complaining about being kicked out tomorrow, so we're leaving tonight?" Simpson asked, baffled by the logic, or the lack of it. "I don't understand."

"You plan on leaving before breakfast?" Briggs asked, incredulous, "knowing as you do Harold's artistry with an egg, not to mention his skill with bacon? Are you feeling all right, Billy-Boy?"

"Never better," Carruthers said expansively. "Blood rushing through the brain a mile a minute, like — like — " He was instantly sorry.

"Like water through a fire hose at a four-alarmer?" Simpson asked.

"Like Piccadilly Pete running from Inspector Morrison just after he heisted the Charity diamond?" Briggs asked, and could not help but add a bit modestly, "That was from one of mine, you know. It was called *Smothered on Saturday* — "

"Stop it!" Carruthers said sharply. "Tim, you and Cliff gather up our effects. Let's move to the library."

"But what has this to do with getting into the cupboard?" Briggs asked.

"Patience," Carruthers said, and his smile became even more enigmatic, if such a thing is possible. "Patience and faith . . . . "

He led the way into the library, saw where the ancient scroll had tumbled from, stood on tiptoe to inspect the dusty niche, and nodded in satisfaction. Had he invented a dusty niche for an opus of his own, he could scarcely have done better than the one facing him. The alcove was also nicely noticeable, and he made sure it remained that way, like a gap tooth in an otherwise even set of plates, by tucking Tim Briggs's epic onto another shelf out of sight.

This portion of Carruthers' plan completed, Billy-Boy now searched for and found the shelf containing reference material while his two friends watched with ill-concealed mystification. Here he located a Britannica and brought it forth, noting with pleasure that it was not the new Micro-Macro unintelligible edition, but an older, more comprehensible one. He ran his fingers along the spines, found the volume that purported to cover subjects ranging from P to Plastering, and brought it down. He opened it, leafing through the pages, and then paused dramatically, his thick finger resting on an entry.

"John Avery," he read aloud, and looked up, his finger holding his place. "That, my friends, is what I meant by patience and faith. I thought the name Avery sounded familiar. When I was at work — admittedly some time back — on a book of mine called *Skulling on the High Seas*, I did quite a bit of research on the miscreants who flew the pirate flag, and the name Avery was rather prominent among them. It is true that Morgan and Blackboard and Kidd and that crew got most of the publicity — and eventually suffered thereby, which should be a lesson to us all — but the really important buccaneers were men such as John Avery, Bartholomew Roberts, Captain Mission, the French corsair, and others of that ilk. John Avery may or may not have been related to the Josephus Avery branch of the family — in fact I rather doubt it — but no matter." He looked about. "Now, who has a fountain pen?"

"A fountain pen?" Simpson asked, now thoroughly confused.

"Exactly!" Carruthers said, pleased to have been understood the first time.

"Are you *sure* you're all right, Billy-Boy?" Briggs asked in a worried tone, but he brought forth his fountain pen just the same.

"I'm fine," Carruthers said, and added hastily, "and please do not give me a litany of comparisons." He acknowledged the pen. "Thank you, Tim. Now, my friends, a bit of x-marks-the-spotting . . . . " He suited the action to the word, placing his x near the intersection of two of the fine lines on the back, his enigmatic smile becoming positively fiendish, which made it, of course, no longer enigmatic. "Now, a bit of dust to hide the fact that this judicious x has not weathered the ages — dust of which, I am pleased to see, the room has more than ample supply . . . . "

He rubbed the spot with dust and stood back to check his work.

"Excellent! What else? Ah, of course, the encyclopedia — back into place and a little more dust to disguise the fact it had ever been disturbed . . . . "

He checked everything once again, and, satisfied, beamed at his companions.

"Billy-Boy," Simpson asked, worried, "would you like to lie down?"

"Later," Carruthers said. "Much later, in most probability."

"But, Billy-Boy," Briggs said imploringly, "what has this to do with the cupboard holding the brandy and champagne?"

Carruthers held the two of his companions with his glittering eye; the Ancient Mariner would have been hard-pressed to come in second in a contest with him.

"Everything!" he said. "And now, my friends, this is exactly what we must do . . . . "

12

When Clarence Wellington Alexander was quite young and taking loot from his fellow classmates that would have been impossible to explain to his parents, he kept his booty in a shoe box as high up on a shelf in his room as he could reach, behind a bottle in which he kept a live frog. He hoped this would prove a deterrent to his mother if she came looking for a shoe box in which to store something for herself, or to lend to a neighbor for a family picnic. It was not the best of hiding places, as Clarence would have been the first to admit, but in their small house with its tiny garden there was no place he could think of that was any better. And, of course, it would have been difficult for a twelve-year-old to rent a safety-deposit box without embarrassing questions being asked. But the situation led to Clarence's being — as Briggs suspected all snide people of being — an extremely light sleeper, coming awake at the first sound of anyone trying the doorknob of his room. The truth was, Clarence Alexander did not get a really good night's rest until his first night in prison.

He did not, however, have to be a particularly light sleeper to be brought abruptly from the arms of Morpheus by the racket that woke him at two o'clock that morning. It seemed to him at first that someone was simultaneously attempting to destroy the front door with an ax or something similar, while someone else was trying to break through either a wall or the floor itself, using a chair as a battering ram. There were also assorted sounds of other breakage of one sort or another.

He was out of his bed in a flash, not pausing for a robe, and was down the steps in an instant, pressing the light switch that controlled the illumination for both the lower hallway and the library. A moment later Harold, not a light sleeper himself, but by the same token also not deaf, joined him, yawning. The scene that greeted the two might have been humorous at another time, resembling as it did one of those comedy vaudeville acts involving inept carpenters that end with the stage set a shambles, but at the moment it looked to Clarence anything but funny. It appeared to him to be highly suspicious.

William Carruthers, fully dressed at that hour, as were his confederates, had apparently fallen over an arm chair in the Stygian darkness, while Timothy Briggs, trying to open the outer door in the dark, had been stumbled over by Clifford Simpson. In stumbling, Simpson had apparently struck his head on the portal and then collapsed over a table, sending it flying; while Briggs's small but hard head, after bouncing off the floor, had apparently been driven into a cane chair, upending it. In the commotion their bags had escaped them, flying through the air, and had contributed their share to the holocaust in the form of untabled lamps and upended footstools.

Clarence glared. "All right!" he said darkly. "What's this all about?"

Billy-Boy managed to struggle to his feet. He tugged his clothing straight and tried to face Clarence with an air of dignity, marred somewhat by his necktie's being halfway around his neck, and with having lost a shoe in his fall, which gave him the attitude of a captain standing on the sloping deck of a sinking ship, addressing the crew.

"Sir," Carruthers said formally, "you informed us last evening in no uncertain manner, that we were no longer welcome in your household. We, sir, have been raised with proper respect for decent standards; we, sir, do not remain where we are not wanted. We were in the process of removing ourselves from the premises, when we had the misfortune to awaken you. If you will return to your sleep with our apologies, we will take our departure again, trying to do it a bit more quietly this time."

"Aw, gee, pops," Harold said in a disappointed tone. He had interpreted enough of Carruthers' statement to understand that when the three old men had inadvertently awakened him, they had been in the process of doing a bunk without saying good-by. "You gave me your word you wouldn't try to escape — "

"My dear Harold," Carruthers said in a kindly tone, "one can hardly call being instructed to leave and never darken a napkin again quite the same thing as escaping." He picked up his bag; both Briggs and Simpson also retrieved theirs. Carruthers bowed slightly at the waist. "And now, gentlemen, if you'll excuse us — "

"Wait a second! Wait a second!" Clarence's eyes narrowed; he studied the three of them with growing suspicion. "Hold it right there! Last night you three characters were begging to stay at any price, as if this was a boarding-house, or a free-lunch counter. You did everything but tie yourselves to the kitchen table, or lock yourselves in the john! And now you want to bust out of here at two in the morning just like that? Who do you think you clowns are kidding?"

Carruthers drew himself up. "Kidding, sir?"

"Kidding!" Clarence said flatly. "Hal, search them!"

Carruthers tried to draw himself even further up and merely came to his tiptoes. He lowered himself in the interests of stability.

"Sir, I consider that an insult! To suggest that we would transgress your hospitality and remove any of your personal possessions after the kindness we have been fortunate enough to receive in this menage! Although in the inter-ests of honesty I must say that those kindnesses came at the hands of Harold, and not yourself. Still, the principle remains, I am afraid. I consider your charge, sir, as calumny!"

"Yes. Well," Clarence said evenly, not greatly impressed by Carruthers' the-atrics, "I'm suggesting that possibly you aren't taking any of my personal pos-sessions, since I've got the key to the liquor cupboard, and I sleep with my wallet under the pillow; but I happen to be responsible for this house and everything in it. It's in the lease, and they have an inventory, and I have enough grief without getting in a hassle with some English lawyer when the time comes for me and Harold to split from here. So, Hal, shake them down."

Harold sighed but moved over to Carruthers. "Gee, I'm sorry, pops," he said apologetically.

"That's perfectly all right," Carruthers said. "It's the only way to still the suspicions of your friend." He put his feet apart and leaned with the palms of his hands against the wall, looking back over his shoulder. "Is this the proper drill? The correct stance?"

"That's fine."

"Good. Just be a bit careful in the stomach area, if you don't mind," Carruthers suggested. "Ticklish, you know."

"I know. Me, too," Harold said. He patted the pockets, ran a hand down the legs, and stepped back. "Pops is clean. And if shorty or skinny had so much as a matchbox on them, it would show, Clare."

"True. Then it must be in their bags," Clarence said shortly, and began by kneeling down and opening Carruthers' old-fashioned valise. His search did not take long; a moment's fumbling within and he looked up triumphantly.

"What's this?" he asked sardonically, and withdrew an oddly shaped package wrapped in a soiled shirt. "Celluloid collars? Button shoes?"

"Hey! Take your hands off that! Be careful how you handle it!" Briggs said suddenly, as if unaware of the contradiction in his statement, and quite as if the words had been forced from him without his will.

"Careful? Believe me I'll be careful!" Clarence said, and slowly unwrapped the package, squatting on his heels. The scroll came into view; Clarence looked up with a smile, but it was not the sort of smile to bring cheer to those viewing it. "This must have grown here like a mushroom, maybe from the dark and the dirty socks," he said with an attempt at humor, "because it sure God wasn't there when I went through this suitcase the night you got here, fatso!" He frowned. "And I'll admit no rolled-up piece of parchment is on the inventory, just dishes, glasses, books, furniture, and garbage like that."

He came to his feet and began circling the library, prepared to move on to the next room and then on to the one after that until the mystery of the scroll was resolved; but he felt it unnecessary when he spotted the gap in the uniformity of the bookshelves. He considered it and nodded his head. The three old men stood like criminals about to be exposed, as Clarence turned to give them a big wink before returning his attention to the gap facing him.

"Well, well!" he said and moved closer to stand on tiptoe to peer into the niche. The marks in the dust were all too apparent, indicating where the parchment had rested, hidden from all eyes for so many generations, behind Briggs's apparently unappreciated — or at least unread — book. Clarence nodded again in complete satisfaction as the puzzle was solved. "So that's where it came from, eh? Back of some piece of junk one of you clowns was lucky enough to pull out, eh?"

"What do you mean, piece of junk?" Briggs said hotly. "I wrote that book!" He was stung to the quick. "What did you ever write?"

"Some of the best oil-stock prospectuses anyone ever read, shorty," Clarence said, and carried the scroll to a lamp. "Let's see what we have here, huh?"

He unrolled the parchment and studied the words with a frown. Quite obviously the thing made little sense to him. He looked up. "All right, what is this thing?" The three faced him in stubborn silence. Clarence's tone hardened. "Look, chums, I asked a question and I expect an answer. Don't make me ask twice; it makes me nervous. For the last time — what is this thing?"

Simpson cleared his throat nervously, preparatory to speaking. Briggs glared at his tall friend.

"Don't tell him a bloody thing, Cliff! We found the scroll; it's ours. Let him find his own bloody scroll. The library may be full of them for all we know."

"Besides, Cliff" — Carruthers' tone suggested that Simpson's normal tendency toward logic be extended to the present circumstances — "Clarence freely admits that the scroll is not a part of his inventory, so he isn't responsible for it. And there's always that old dictum in law: *Qui aliquid repent, tenet; qui amittit, illacrimat."*

Clarence looked at him uncertainly. "What's that supposed to mean?"

"Losers weepers, finders keepers. Probably not the best translation, but adequate, I believe." Carruthers shrugged and held out his hand. "So, if you don't mind, we'd like our scroll back and then we'll leave you in peace."

Clarence took a deep breath. His voice became dangerous.

"I don't think you really realize your position. It may be true that Hal might have some compunction about harming old baggy-pants, here, but I don't think he'd mind much if I asked him to pound shorty into the ground like a tent-stake. And I'm going to do just that in about two seconds flat, if I don't get a straight answer from one of you. Now, *what is this thing?"*

Carruthers sighed, the sigh of one who has done his best but must still face defeat.

"I suppose you'd best tell him, Clifford; if, that is, we do not wish to spend the balance of the night in idle conversation before we are free to leave this place."

"I'm against telling him a bloody thing!" Briggs said belligerently.

"You shut up!" Clarence turned to glare at Simpson. "Well?"

Simpson looked unhappy. "If you insist, sir, but — I'm afraid you won't believe me — "

"Try me!"

"Sir — it seems so ridiculous — "

"I've got a great feeling for the ridiculous," Clarence said coldly, "but not very much patience. *What is this thing?"*

"Yes, sir. It's — " Clifford Simpson wet his lips. He seemed a bit perturbed to be giving such insignificant trivia to a man of Clarence's perspicacity, but then realized there was nothing else for it. "Well, sir, the fact is it's simply a diploma for a man who graduated from Cambridge University after successfully fulfilling the requirements to receive a degree in" — he swallowed — "pig-farming . . . . "

"*What!"*

"Yes, sir. Pig-farming. Or pig-raising, if you wish. The wording of the diploma isn't exactly clear on that point. The word for 'farming' — "

"Oh, so we've got a funny man in the crowd, eh?" Clarence smiled coldly, a smile confined to his thin lips. He studied the heiroglyphics on the parchment again for a moment and then raised his eyes. "Hal — "

Harold's head came up with a jerk; he had been dozing on his feet. "Yeah, Clare?"

"Take skinny, here, outside and see if you can fit him into the rain barrel. If you have to tear off an arm or a leg to tuck him in, don't worry about it!"

"Wait a moment," Carruthers said hastily. He looked at his two friends apologetically. "Sorry, Tim. Sorry, Cliff. There's nothing for it, I'm afraid, except to tell him what he wants to hear. Otherwise — " He shrugged. "Still," he added, "there should be plenty in it for everyone, as far as that goes . . . . "

"Plenty of what in what for who?" Clarence asked suspiciously.

"I believe that should be 'for whom,'" Carruthers said critically, and frowned. "Or possibly not. I was never sure about that one. But no matter. Plenty of money, sir, money! For all of us." His tone became stern, he looked Clarence in the eye. "And I'm afraid I must be adamant about that provision. A fair distribution, that is."

"Money?" Clarence stared at the parchment.

"Yes. You see," Carruthers said, putting as much conviction in his voice as he could, "the fact is that that parchment is simply a map. The map is on the reverse side, with instructions for its use on the face of the document. The map itself is very faint — you can barely make it out, but it's still visible enough, fortunately. It was foolish of this man Avery to place the map on the outside, but I expect he felt the instructions were equally as important as the map itself. Certainly one would have been useless without the other. But, you see, some of these old-time pirates — "

"Chee!" Harold said, coming awake, his eyes gleaming. "A pirate map!"

"Wait a second! Hold the phone!" Clarence looked at the parchment again, studying both sides with care, and then looked up, a sardonic smile on his lips. "What are you trying to do? Sell me a pirate map? A *pirate map?* To *me?*" He shook his head. "Man, I'm the expert on con games. A pirate map, yet, in this day and age! You should be ashamed!"

"Sir," Simpson said, reaching out a long arm and pointing, "do you see the name Avery there? Do you deny this is the Avery farm? And surely anyone can see the lines on the back appear to be a map of some sort, at least if the words mean anything. And that tiny letter x, which obviously marks some sort of spot?"

Clarence's smile widened.

"Well, I have to give you credit for being a trifle better than rank amateurs," he said, a slight tone of congratulation in his voice, "but take my word for it, you're still amateurs. So you discovered the coincidence of the names and thought you could con me with it, eh? Selling pirate maps! Gentlemen, pirate maps went out with the Spanish prisoner gag, or with gold bricks. Today it's oil wells, or even bridges. But pirate maps?" He sneered. "A good try, gents, but no cigar."

Carruthers sighed mightily, looking crestfallen.

"Yes. Well," he said regretfully, "it was all I could think up on the spur of the moment, since you would not accept the truth of its being just a diploma for pig-farming. And I could scarcely stand by and see Clifford come to harm without some effort on my part. I was afraid you would not be taken in, but one doesn't win them all. Unfortunately." He shook his head at his poor luck in convincing Clarence, and held out his hand. "And now, sir, if we could please have our diploma back, we'll be on our way."

"Now, hold it!" Clarence said with irritation. "You aren't going anywhere!"

For a moment he wondered if possibly that was the idea; to get him to allow them to stay a few extra days, but he doubted it. If they stayed they would stay without any brandy and champagne, and with the bare minimum of food, and they must have known that would be the case. No; apparently they truly wished to leave with the parchment, and until he knew for sure exactly what the thing was, they were going to stay right here if he had to nail their shoes to the floor! He could, of course, let them leave without the parchment, but they already knew what the thing said, so that was out. He glanced at Harold, about to ask if by any chance the large man could read the thing, but he knew this was ridiculous.

"Hal — first thing in the morning I want you to get over to the nearest school and bring me back a professor who can read this thing. Understand?"

"It's Latin," Simpson said helpfully. "That should limit your search."

"Don't tell him a thing!" Briggs said angrily.

"Shut up. A Latin professor," Clarence said. "Understand? Bring him back."

"You mean, snatch him?" Harold asked. He looked disturbed. "Gee, Clare, we ain't got no more beds, and we're runnin' low on sheets. And I don't know no five-handed card games — "

"No, stupid! Not snatch him! Or maybe I'd better go myself if I want to get somebody who knows what I'm talking about, and you guys can play four-handed potsie!" He turned to the three old men. "I'm going to find out what this is all about, believe me! I figure this thing must have some value, since the three of you characters are so anxious to get out of here with it — "

"Hey, Clare!" Harold had come up with another thought, his second in a week, and he was proud of it.

"Now, what is it?" Clarence asked, irritated.

"Hey, supposin' it's like pops says, a real pirate map," Harold said, his brain now as awake as it ever got, and bumping along on the rails. "Or supposin' even if it ain't a pirate map, but it still says somethin' on it that maybe means dough, which even you think maybe it does. Now, supposin' one of us gets ahold of this professor to come here and read the thing. How do we know he's goin' to tell us the truth? How do we know he ain't goin' to come up with some story like it's just an old shoppin' list, or a laundry bill, or somethin' like that? And then he goes out and collects on what it really says in the thing. What about that?"

It was a long speech, even for Harold, who enjoyed talking. Clarence had been listening to the exposition with growing concern for his own sagacity, of which he had always been so proud. Harold had raised a perfectly legitimate point, and one he should have thought of himself. Possibly it was the lateness of the hour that was fogging his mind, or at least he hoped so. He would hate to think he was losing his touch to the extent that he had to take suggestions from a meat-head like Harold.

Still, what was the answer? Surely there had to be someone in the entire British Isles who was knowledgeable enough in Latin to translate the gibberish for him, and who could still be trusted. But who? He became aware that Carruthers was mumbling something that was disturbing his concentration, and looked up, irritated.

"What?"

"Solicitors — lawyers to you, of course," Carruthers was saying.

"What about them?"

"I merely said that I shall see my solicitors regarding this situation," Carruthers said coldly. "My solicitors look most unfavorably upon people having their rightful possessions taken from them without due process. Solicitors — lawyers, that is, as I believe I've already mentioned — frown upon such things. Lawyers — solicitors, that is — "

"Ah, shut up!" Clarence said impolitely, and went back to his pondering. That old buzzard and his prattling about lawyers, lawyers, lawyers! He ought to — wait a second! Hold the phone! A lawyer — that really wasn't a bad idea, now that he thought about it. Lawyers and judges, they had to know Latin, didn't they? And they were sworn to uphold the law, so they had to be honest — or relatively honest, anyway. And if they made the dough here in England that lawyers raked in back home, they wouldn't be as hungry as some professor who was probably starving to death. He ought to thank old baggy-pants for having given him the idea.

But where to find a lawyer, and one who was guaranteed to have enough scratch to be — relatively — honest. Where?

"Phew!" Simpson said suddenly. "It's hot in here!"

"Phew, indeed," Briggs said, agreeing. "P.U., in fact. It also smells."

"Keep quiet — " Clarence began, and then paused. What other lawyer than the one mentioned in that newspaper article about the three old men? What was his name? Pugh! That was it, Sir Percival Pugh! The article said he demanded and received the highest fees, so that should mean he ought to have enough money not to cheat a couple of visitors to British shores like Clarence and Harold. Oh, sure, he'd give the guy a decent fee for translating the thing, but it would be worth it. Pugh! He turned and smiled at Carruthers, a chilling smile.

"Okay, fatso," he said, his tone precluding the slightest argument, "now, here's the way we're going to play it. Tomorrow morning first thing you're going to write a note to an old friend of yours — this Sir Percival Pugh. I don't care what you say, but it better be good, because I don't want any argument from him. I want him to come back here with Harold and translate that thing. And don't get cute in what you write," he added direly, "because I'm going to be reading every word over your shoulder while you write it." He suddenly grinned, a savage grin. "You wanted a lawyer; well, you're going to get one."

"We don't want Pugh!" Briggs said forcefully. "We — "

"You'll take what you get and like it," Clarence said, and his smile went as quickly as it had come. He looked over at Harold. "Hal, put our guests back to bed. And you sleep in a chair in front of their door in case any of them gets to walking in his sleep and picks up some more of the Avery estate. This — " he held up the scroll — "goes to bed with me." His smile came back briefly. "Good night, then, gentlemen. Pleasant dreams . . . . "

"Well," Briggs said, "it was lucky that Harold raised the point about the possibility of an outside professor's being venal, rather than our raising it, as planned." They were back in the privacy of their bed chamber. Carruthers had changed again into his horrendous pajamas and was lying quite contentedly on his bed. From beyond the door they could hear the reassuring snores of Harold, propped in a chair across the sill.

"Yes," Carruthers said, "it just goes to prove that even the blindest sow finds an acorn now and then."

"Agreed," Simpson said with a faint smile. He looked over at Briggs. "You don't really mind old Pugh being involved, do you?"

Briggs laughed. "Lord, no! My objection in the library was purely cosmetic. To lock in Clarence's decision. Actually," he said, "this is one time I think old Pugh's abilities might come in handy for us. And about time, too!" he added darkly under his breath, and rolled over to go to sleep.

"It reminds me of a plot I used in one of my earliest endeavors," Simpson said nostalgically. "It was called *Strychnine in the Solicitor*, I believe, or did we finally end up calling it *Arsenic in the Advocate*? I know it was one or the other; they were the only two we considered. At any rate, it dealt with — "

He became aware that the snores of his two companions had joined those of Harold in an almost hypnotic chorus, and with a sigh he rolled over to seek slumber himself.

13

Dear Herr Pugh:

("Pugh comes from German aristocracy, you know," Carruthers explained, "and is very fussy about how he's addressed." "Be as polite as you want," Clarence said, "just get him here!" "Yes, sir," Carruthers said, and went back to his composing.)

A very good Germanic morning to you, sir. You may recall we met when you defended my good friend, Clifford Simpson, before Sir Bartholomew Roberts when Clifford was accused of murder. I can still remember how you made a young goat out of the Prosecutor; you certainly were able to teach him a thing or two!

("Sir Percival loves flattery," Carruthers explained. "That's all in there to put him in a good mood, to make him receptive." "Spread it on with a trowel if it makes him happy," Clarence said, reading over his shoulder, "just get him here!" "Right," Carruthers said, and went on.)

My reason for writing is that we have come into possession of a rather interesting bit of parchment which we feel could benefit from your expert interpretation.

If you would be so kind as to accompany the gentleman who presents this note, I am sure we would be most appreciative. There will be a payment for your time, of course.

I know you prefer traveling in a German Karte, but unfortunately, all the man has is an English car.

A very good day to you, sir.

Sincerely,
William Carruthers.

("How's that?" Carruthers asked. "Satisfactory?" "It is if it brings him here," Clarence said flatly, folding the note and tucking it into its envelope. "Otherwise it's garbage." "I assure you it will bring him," Carruthers said. "You have my word for it." "That and a dime will get you coffee," Clarence said brusquely, and came to his feet, raising his voice. "Hall")

Sir Percival Pugh was a handsome, well-built man in his middle forties, a trifle above average in height, with extremely sharp dark blue eyes which he could mask with innocence at a moment's notice, with fair hair combed a bit longer than the style over a wide brow that had a slight bulge, as if requiring the additional room for the massive intelligence lodged behind it. Sir Percival had just completed a late breakfast and had gone into his study to practice his card tricks — for prestidigitation and amateur magic were two of Sir Percival's most ardent hobbies — when his butler appeared to announce they had a visitor with a message for Sir Percival which he refused to hand over to any surrogate.

The butler's tone indicated (a) that if the visitor had to appear at all, he should have used the servants' entrance rather than the front hall; (b) that the visitor should have parked that sad example of the automobilemaker's art around the corner rather than in his lordship's driveway where people might see it and think it pertained to the house; and (c) that if he, the butler, that is, had raised any of these points with the visitor, it would have been suicidal. Sir Percival, well accustomed to reading both his butler's tone as well as his expression, frowned and bade the butler to allow the gentleman in. He then sat back and awaited developments.

After his butler's unspoken comments, Sir Percival was really not surprised when Harold appeared in the doorway, clutching the note in one large, sweating hand. This was, of course, the large man who had hustled William Carruthers into that wretched little car at the airport; the muscle in the kidnaping. He was here, therefore, with a note from Carruthers, since there was no other possible link between them. He accepted the note from Harold, and glanced first at the signature, not at all surprised that he had been correct in his surmise; Sir Percival was not accustomed to being wrong. He was pleased to see that although the kidnapers had obviously learned by now that Carruthers and his friends were penniless, at least they had not punished him for his poverty. Or at least they had not broken his arms, since he was able to write. Well, possibly the note might further clarify the situation. He went back to the top of the page and began reading.

His first feeling was one of irritation at Carruthers. Pugh's family was about as Germanic as Yorkshire pudding; he could trace his ancestry back eighteen generations in Wales and a few centuries in Ireland before that. He understood the necessity for this fiction, however, in order for Carruthers to bring up the German *Morgen* for morning, obviously the closest poor Carruthers had been able to come to the name "Morgan." He even forgave Carruthers the "young goat" for Kidd, and the use of Bartholomew Roberts' name, when actually Lord Justice Pomeroy had presided at Simpson's trial. But when the man went to such infantile lengths to bring in the name "Teach," it was too much! It was a wonder he hadn't said something about a witness with a black beard! And that "A very — " at the end was the final straw!

Pugh was a man who required extremely few clues; his mammoth brain rebelled at having too many hints thrust at it, as if suggesting that his giant intellect needed them to solve any mystery. Still, the hints had gone over the head of the brains behind the kidnaping — for Sir Percival had known from the day at the airport that the large man in the room with him had only been the muscle — but it was still taking chances to put so much down on paper, and Pugh disliked any unnecessary chances.

He went back and read the note a second time, although its message was firmly imprinted on his brain. German Karte, indeed! So obviously Carruthers had unearthed some bit of parchment which was a pirate map, or which pur- ported to be a pirate map, or which — most probably — was neither, but which Carruthers wished him to authenticate as a pirate map, no matter what it was. At that moment Sir Percival could not see where there was any profit in it for him — the mention of a fee did not sound substantial — and profit for Sir Percival came first in all his calculations. On the other hand, Carruthers should have been well aware of this trait of Sir Percival's character, and should scarcely have written the note to him without taking this factor into account. In any event, he had nothing else to do that afternoon, and it would be pleasant to see Billy-Boy Carruthers again. But first he wished more information, and went about getting it in the manner he knew best. He smiled genially at Harold.

"One word, if I may," he said politely. "There is mention in this note of payment for my services. You'll pardon me for being frank, but in all honesty —
while I am sure your other attributes outshine this minor failing — you do not
look as if you could afford to pay a very large fee."

Harold had been standing first on one foot and then on the other, quite
uncomfortable in this fine house, but Sir Percival's words brought him from
his embarrassment.

"Me? I ain't goin' to pay nothin'," he said disdainfully. "If you're lookin' for
dough, you better look to Clare."

"Clare? Your wife?"

"Naw! Clarence, my partner. I just call him Clare for short, like he calls me
Hal. Well," Harold added, some of Simpson's tendency toward honesty having rubbed off on him the past day or so, "he's actually more my boss than a
partner. Mainly on account of he's got all the dough."

"As good a reason as any and better than most, as I'm sure any captain of
industry would agree. But when you say, in your quaint fashion, that your
friend has — and I quote — 'all the dough,' does that mean he had sufficient
to pay me a reasonable fee?"

"Who, Clare?" Harold waved away any doubts with one of his basket-sized
hands. "He's got enough unless you're out of your mind for what you charge."

"Oh?" Sir Percival sounded dubious.

"Yeah! Clare's got almost sixty grand stashed away in a safe at the house.
He thinks I don't know, but I do. As if I couldn't open that box with a piece of
boiled spaghetti the worst day I ever seen! Only thing is," he added sadly, "I
wouldn't rob Clare. He's my partner."

"An admirable sentiment," Pugh said graciously, "and one that does you
credit." Almost sixty grand, the man said; roughly thirty thousand pounds.
And this naughty man Clarence was greedy enough to try to get more by
kidnaping an elderly gentleman. Well, Pugh thought, possibly we can teach
this Clarence the error of his ways — at a slight charge, of course. But
lessons of that nature never came cheap; if they did, people would never
learn. It would take a bit of planning, but Pugh had no doubts on that score.
He looked up.

"I'll be a few minutes. Would you care for a cup of coffee in the kitchen?"

"Gee, sure!" Harold said wholeheartedly. He had been ill at ease in the
room, whose carpeting seemed to be as thick as the jute piles at Sing Sing.
The kitchen, he was sure, was equally well appointed, but it would be more
his style.

"Fine," Pugh said, and rang for the butler. As he watched Harold lumber
from the room, his eyes narrowed and his giant brain began to consider the
delicate edifice of the plan he was constructing. As each wall went into place,

he nodded, checked it for stability, and then moved on to the next step. And when at last the carpeting had been laid and the pictures neatly hung on the walls and properly straightened, he came to his feet and walked into his library. He located his file of newspapers, selected one a week old, checked it over carefully, and smiled. He then packed his briefcase with the necessary materials, added the newspaper, and walked into the kitchen.

"Ready," he said to Harold.

"Great!" Harold said, relieved to be quit of the luxurious mansion. "The car's in the drive . . . . "

The three elderly gentlemen were seated around the kitchen table playing cards, but the card play without the aid of brandy and champagne, and with no money involved — not to mention playing with cards whose backs were known to all — was desultory to say the least. At the sound of Harold opening the front door, they all looked up in anticipation. Carruthers threw down his cards and came to his feet; the others followed suit, trailing him into the library, where Harold had ushered his guest.

"Ah, Sir Percival!" Carruthers said warmly.

"Mr. Carruthers! And Mr. Briggs and Mr. Simpson, too." Pugh was actually not surprised to see them all there, nor did it affect his plan except in the most minor of details. His computerlike brain had already noted the facts and was in the process of handing down a print-out. Obviously a ransom note had been sent to the two at their club, and Briggs, most likely, had come to the spot where the ransom was to be delivered, probably carrying a bag with fresh clothing for Carruthers, since (a) they had no money, and (b) the shirt Carruthers was wearing seemed to be relatively clean, even if excessively patterned. And, not having any money, Briggs had also been taken into custody and a second ransom note had undoubtedly been dispatched, probably asking for twice as much, and poor Simpson, not having a clue as to what to do, had shown up and spilled the beans as to the financial bind they found themselves in. And when Clarence had tried to send them about their business as a lost cause, the three — or, more likely, Carruthers — had come up with this parchment business. Which, Pugh said to himself in satisfaction, brings us up to today's breathtaking episode; come next Saturday and bring sixpence. All of the above ratiocination having taken but a fraction of a second, he continued speaking seemingly without pause. "And how are you all keeping?"

"Fine!" Carruthers said with a wide smile, answering for them all. "The reason we asked you here — "

"Quiet! No hints!" Clarence said sternly, and came forward to introduce himself. "Sir Percival, my name is Clarence — "

"Alexander. I know," Sir Percival said in a kindly tone. "Harold was good enough to do the introductions while we were driving here. How do you do, sir?"

"I'll do a lot better once you translate something in Latin for me," Clarence said, and turned to glare at the three. "And like I said, no hints!" He turned back to Sir Percival, bringing the scroll to the table and unrolling it. He pointed. "Here you are, Sir Percival. Just what is this thing?"

Pugh bent over the table looking profoundly studious. In his mind's eye he could see little Briggs crossing his fingers behind his back, and could imagine Simpson wetting his lips nervously, but he was equally sure that Billy-Boy Carruthers was looking as unconcerned and benign as ever. Patience and faith! Pugh thought with an inner smile, and brought his attention back to the parchment. He nodded slowly.

"Remarkable!" he murmured. "May I?" He took the scroll carefully and turned it over, studying the hairline cracks on the back and raising his eyebrows spectacularly at seeing the x imprinted there. He then reversed the parchment once more and continued reversing it as he compared the words on one side with the tiny lines on the other. "Truly amazing! I should not have thought it possible!"

"Yes, that's fine, but what *is* it?" At this point Clarence was almost pleading.

"Ah, yes, that's why you called me here, wasn't it? Well," Sir Percival said in a scholarly tone, "to be brief, it appears to be a map of some sort, and a reference on the other side to a treasure this map purports to locate." His eyes came up from the scroll and he took a deep breath. "It seems hard to believe, after all these years and with so many people searching for it through the centuries, but it appears to be the key to the Great Mogul treasure!"

Clarence leaned forward, his eyes bulging. "Are you sure?"

"Quite. One could scarcely make a mistake about a thing like that, could one?" Sir Percival put down the scroll with a sigh and smiled genially. "Yes. And now, if you don't mind, possibly you could pay me — considering the small amount of work involved in the translation, plus the pleasure you have given me in permitting me to look upon this famous document, I think fifty pounds should do — and then could Harold drive me home? I'm expecting some friends over this afternoon for a few hands of bridge."

"Hey!" Harold said enthusiastically. "You play — ?"

"Hal, shut up!" Clarence said crossly. "Sir Percival — "

"Yes?"

"I — I — " Clarence was torn. Obviously one did not snatch people like Sir Percival Pugh. Harold had undoubtedly left fingerprints all over Sir Percival's home when he was there, as well as probably parking in the drive where everyone could see and later identify the car. Besides, if Sir Percival

Pugh were missing it would be quite a different matter from those three old nobodies. In Sir Percival's case all Scotland Yard would be involved, and the cops would be here as soon as they could trace the large man with whom Sir Percival had left his home. And Clarence needed a covey of cops around about as much as he needed an impacted wisdom tooth.

On the other hand, what good was a genuine pirate map if he couldn't decipher it? No. He had to get Sir Percival to tell him what the parchment said before he left. But how? Clarence cleared his throat.

"Sir Percival," he said, "we — well, we more or less assumed it was a map of some sort, a pirate map of some sort, that is — " Clarence was trying his best to sound sincere while at the same time attempting to broadcast a threat to any who might be tempted to contradict him, no easy chore. "It's just — well, we were hoping you would tell us a bit more — "

"More? But there really isn't much more to be told," Sir Percival said, sounding puzzled by the request. "As we both agree, it is a pirate map. Quite old and genuine in every respect, as far as I can judge, and relating, in my opinion, to the location of the Great Mogul treasure, lost all these years. And now, if you really don't mind, I would like transportation back to my home. Guests this afternoon, you know," he added a trifle apologetically.

"Wait a second!" Clarence said desperately. The old men also knew what the map said, but after their trying to con him the night before with that diploma for pig-farming nonsense — pig-farming, yet! — he wouldn't trust their interpretation any further than he could kick a Sherman tank uphill against the wind.

"Yes?" Sir Percival said politely.

"Ah — well, look, Sir Percival," Clarence said, trying to make up his mind without quite knowing what he wanted to make up his mind about. "What I mean is — well, what I figured I'd get for your fee — well, what do the words actually say?"

"Just what I've just finished telling you," Sir Percival said with the air of one whose patience is not limitless. He withdrew a pocket watch and looked at it rather pointedly.

"At least, does it say how big the treasure is?" Clarence asked, almost wailing, picking at straws.

Sir Percival paused and then nodded, as if Clarence had raised an interesting point. He checked his watch again, seemed to come to the conclusion that he still had several minutes before he had to run, and seated himself comfortably in a chair.

"Now, that's a rather fascinating subject for conjecture," he said musingly. "Although I believe we can make some decent assumptions, and come to some rather startling conclusions. We can assume, for example, with every degree of accuracy, that the J. Avery mentioned in the scroll is none other than the famous — or, rather, infamous — pirate, John Avery. We can make this deduction since this is the Avery farm, and since the scroll was hidden here. And also — although I suppose I should not be telling you this — the scroll apparently is based upon one of his major acts of piracy — "

("I tried to tell you about that Avery bit," Simpson said to Clarence reproachfully, "but you wouldn't listen." "Shut up," Clarence said uncharitably. "Go on, Sir Percival.")

"Yes. Well," Sir Percival said, tenting his fingers and contemplating them all over them, "we know that John Avery, alias Every, alias Bridgeman, and also known among the fraternity as Long Ben and the Arch-Pirate, was born in this general vicinity, give or take a hundred miles or so, and went to sea as a youth in the merchant marine. This was not, of course, uncommon among youths at the time, but what was a bit unusual, possibly, was that after becoming a mate, John Avery led a mutiny and took the crew and ship into piracy. He was quite active as well as being successful — the two are not always synonymous — but his major stroke was the famous prize he took in the Red Sea, a ship, as I've stated before, of the Great Mogul. And on that ship, and a treasure never seen since, was a booty of" — he paused for effect — "100,000 gold pieces of eight . . . . "

Clarence gulped. "How — how much is that in today's money?"

Sir Percival considered, a slight frown accompanying his calculations.

"Let us see. The piece of eight has been considered by some to be named for a coin which was the equivalent of eight *reales*. Others — and for the purposes of this discussion I throw my weight in this direction — thought of it as the *dobl—n de ocho* of the Spain of the era, the doubloon of eight escudo of gold, as we call it. Its weight was a trifle under twenty-eight grams, or approximately one ounce in today's scale."

Clarence was stunned. One thing he knew very well was numbers; another was money.

"One hundred thousand ounces of gold? *One hundred thousand ounces of gold?*" He took a deep breath, trying to control the trembling that had begun to take him in its grip. "At over two hundred dollars an ounce? That's — that's *twenty million dollars!*" He leaned toward Pugh. "Where is it? *Where is it?*"

Sir Percival shook his head regretfully.

"I'm afraid that was not in our deal. You wished to know what the parchment represented. I have told you. And now, if you and Harold are both busy, possibly you might at least drive me to the train? After paying my fee, of course."

"Hold it! Hold it!" The thought of losing twenty million dollars was, in itself, unthinkable. Clarence tried to bring his whirling thoughts to some sort of order. Twenty million bucks! Twenty million smackeroos! That old man Carruthers had sure been right when he said there was enough for them all! But that didn't mean that any of it had to be thrown away! And to think it all started because Harold picked up a newspaper someone had left in a bar, which in turn had led him to kidnaping the old man for a paltry twenty grand! Old Opportunity had done himself proud, this time! He brought himself back to earth, swallowing. "Look, Sir Percival. There's plenty for everyone. After all, I showed you the scroll. It wouldn't be right for you to try to cut me out of the deal."

Sir Percival considered Clarence for several moments. Then, at last, and with a sigh, he made up his mind.

"Possibly you are right," he said. "Legally, for your information, you haven't a leg to stand on. You not only showed me the scroll, as you yourself have just now stated, but you even offered me a fee to read it — a fee, I might mention, which has yet to be paid. But in a moral sense, I expect you have a point. However, since I now know where the treasure is — and you do not — and since I can move quite quickly when necessary, I suggest that my portion be seventy-five per cent, and yours be the balance."

"Wait a second!" Briggs said hotly. "What about us? After all, Billy-Boy thought of — " He seemed to realize what he was saying. "I mean," he said a bit sheepishly, since he had to say something, "we found the scroll in the first place."

Again Sir Percival considered.

"I suppose there is some justice in what you say," he said, and tried to be fair about the matter. "What about seventy-five per cent for me, and you three and Clarence and Harold to divide the other twenty-five per cent. After all," he pointed out, "that would be five per cent each, which is not to be caviled at, considering the sum of money we are talking about."

"Wait a second!" Clarence said angrily. "There's only one of you, and two of us!"

"And three of us," Carruthers pointed out. He was beginning to enjoy himself.

"And those old men know what's on the parchment, too," Clarence added angrily. "You're not the only one can read Latin!"

"True. I should have expected that Simpson, at least, and also possibly Carruthers, would be familiar with the translation," Pugh said sadly, while Briggs bridled at being left out. "A problem . . . " Sir Percival pursed his lips and closed his eyes, as if to better plan a fair and equitable distribution of the huge sum of money. At last he opened his eyes. "You drive a hard bargain. We'll do it this way," he said, his regret at giving up such a large share of the money evident in his voice. "Since we are, in effect, three interested parties, we'll divide the money into three equal portions. One third, of course, to me;

one third to Clarence and Harold, and one third to Mr. Carruthers and his two friends."

Clarence was about to object again, when he realized that once they all had their individual shares, he could easily kidnap one of the old men again — anyone but that big-mouthed runt, Briggs — and end up with a good portion of their share as well.

"Okay," he said brusquely. "Now, what does that thing say?"

Sir Percival held up an admonitory hand.

"One moment," he said. "I believe in cases such as this it is customary to make some gesture to indicate the good faith of the parties involved."

"*Now* what do you mean?" Clarence was beginning to get irked with these constant interruptions that were preventing him from getting at the treasure as soon as possible.

"What I mean is quite simple," Sir Percival said easily. "In cases such as this, since we intend to share a considerable amount of money in three equal parts, some gesture — usually in the form of an equal contribution of money — is made by all three parties."

"Money? How much money?" Clarence asked, instantly-suspicious.

"I believe in the usual agreements, it is normal to place a small percentage of the sum involved in the joint venture, donated in equal parts by each of the partners, in someone's safekeeping. Should, then, any partner fail to demonstrate his good faith, his portion is forfeit, to be divided between the others."

"Yeah," Clarence said, his eyes narrowed, "but how much?"

Sir Percival considered.

"Let me see . . . . In this case, since we are discussing a matter of approximately twenty million dollars, or about seven million dollars plus to each party, I would suggest we each put up half-of-one per cent of our share."

Clarence frowned darkly.

"That's over thirty-five grand! That's a lot of dough." His eyes narrowed as he added the most important thing. "And exactly who holds all that dough?"

"Anyone can hold it," Sir Percival said, and added modestly, "I'll hold it, if you wish."

"*Wait a second —* "

"Or," Pugh said, "if this presents itself to you as a problem, you can hold it. It really makes little difference." He frowned as he made a calculation. "Let us make it an even forty thousand dollars each, or twenty thousand pounds. I see you have a safe here. In that case I suggest you take charge of the money. I assume that is agreeable?"

Clarence thought about it. Despite his natural tendency to be suspicious, he could see nothing wrong with the arrangement, as long as the money was in his safekeeping.

"Yeah. Well, all right."

"That is, if you have your share to begin with," Pugh added significantly.

Clarence glanced at Harold and wished the large man was out of the room. But he could not let the opportunity pass; old O would never forgive him if he did. "I've got my share right here in the house," he said. "What about you?"

"My bank has a branch at East Westerly, which is not far," Sir Percival said. "If you care to drive me there, I can easily arrange the money in a matter of minutes."

Clarence still saw flaws. "What about the old men? You got real generous and cut them in, but they can't come up with the ante. They're broke. So how about cutting them right out again?"

Sir Percival looked at Clarence pityingly.

"You are obviously not familiar with Mr. Carruthers and his rather odd sense of humor," Sir Percival said, and smiled brightly. "I am sure he was pulling your leg when he said they were without funds. It's a habit of his, you know, especially where money is concerned." He looked at Carruthers a trifle sternly. "You really shouldn't do that, Carruthers. It's bad form, you know."

"I — " Billy-Boy was looking confused.

"And don't try to look as if you didn't know exactly what I'm speaking of! Tell the truth, Carruthers! Do you deny that you invested the money you gained from the Jarvis award in Namibian Chartered Mines, Limited?"

"No. I mean, I don't deny it," Carruthers said, amazed at Pugh's knowledge, "but — "

"I thought so," Pugh said rebukingly, interrupting smoothly. "And am I mistaken that you have a mistrust of banks, so that you normally carry the certificates on your person in a money belt?" His eagle eye had noted the slightly larger bulge at Carruthers' stomach and had instantly fed it into the computer.

"Why, yes," Carruthers said, finally beginning to get the message. He only hoped that Briggs and Simpson would also see the light and keep their mouths shut. He opened his shirt, raised the flap of the money belt, and withdrew the certificates. "Here they are."

"So you three clowns were broke, huh?" Clarence was fuming. "You double-crossing, lying, cheating — !" He grabbed the certificates from Carruthers' hand, studied them a moment, and then looked up, his eyes hard. "Who's got a newspaper?"

"By the oddest of coincidences," Sir Percival said, pleased to contribute, "I just happen to have one in my bag." He brought it forth and handed it over, adding a bit apologetically, "I'm afraid it's a few days old . . . . "

"If it's got the stock market reports, that's all I want," Clarence said brusquely, and leafed through the pages until he found the one he wanted.

His finger slid impatiently down the long column of figures. "Namibian Chartered Mines, Limited. Listed at eighteen shillings. And you've got — " He counted and looked up, a dangerous gleam in his eyes. "These certificates are worth over *forty grand!* And you said you were *broke!*"

Carruthers shrugged philosophically.

"Wealth," he said, with a professorial air, "is a relative matter. To one person forty thousand dollars may be a veritable fortune, beyond the wildest dreams of avarice. To another, more fortunate one, forty thousand dollars, particularly in today's economy, may be a mere bagatelle." He frowned thoughtfully. "What was it Shakespeare said?"

"You mean, 'a rose by any other name'?" Simpson asked.

"Or 'a fool and his money'?" Briggs asked.

"Or 'no profit grows where is no pleasure ta'en'?"

"Or, 'our purses shall be proud, our garments poor'?"

"Something like one or all of those," Carruthers said, "or possibly not. No matter." He pointed to the certificates in Clarence's hand. "That is our share in the venture. Consider us in."

"And if you'll be so kind as to drive me to the bank," Sir Percival said, "I shall add my widow's mite to the pile, and then we'll be off and running."

"Okay; but Hal, you keep an eye on these chiseling sharpies until we get back, huh?" Clarence said, and sneered inwardly. So much for all the newspaper talk about the loyalty of one of the old buzzards for the others! He had seen the look of shock on the open countenance of Simpson; it was obvious old skinny had not known the value of those stock certificates; old baggypants was simply a crook! Well, when this was over and he snatched Carruthers a second time, there was no doubt of what he would do with the old man once he had stripped him clean. It was going to be down the well or under the barn, one or the other. Definitely! Lie to him, would they? They must think they were dealing with some clod from the corn belt!

Carruthers cleared his throat, this time suggestively.

"While you are gone," he said, a tentative note in his voice, "since we are now working together for the common weal, I don't suppose you could ease up a bit on the alcohol restrictions . . . ?"

Clarence stared a moment, and then, with a sigh, he tossed the key to the cupboard in Harold's direction. What were a few drinks when a fortune was to be made? Besides, it would likely be the old buzzard's last meal — or last drink — before he went down the hall to the little green door. Once Pugh had been paid off and went his way, it was going to be bread and water for old fatso until D-Day; which would actually be a break for Harold. There would be less excavation to dig the old buzzard's grave. He turned to Sir Percival.

"Okay," he said flatly. "Let's go."

Sir Percival stacked the forty thousand dollars that Clarence had given him, added his own twenty thousand pounds fresh from the bank — they had decided not to be picayune regarding the difference in exchange rates — placed the stock certificates from Carruthers on top, and neatly wrapped the entire amount in some brown paper taken from his bag.

"There," he said with satisfaction, and turned to Clarence. "And now, since it is your desire to be the guardian of the funds, if you would be so kind as to open the safe?"

"Sure," Clarence said, and bent to fiddle with the dial, making sure that his back blocked out any possibility of any of the others noting the combination. He pulled back the outer door, took the packet from Pugh, slid it into an inner alcove, and closed the heavy outer door of the safe.

"Wait a second!" Briggs said suspiciously. "We all have money in there, but Clarence is the only one with the combination!"

"Faith," Sir Percival said reproachfully. "Patience and faith."

"Yeah!" Clarence said. He grinned and twisted the dial.

"Yes," Sir Percival said, and smiled at the others. "We are now, it appears, in business. And with the crass financial considerations taken care of, suppose we get down to the business of the meeting and reveal what the parchment scroll actually says . . . . ."

14

The scroll was before them, unrolled with its message side up:

PRAESES ET CURATORES UNIVERSITATIS
CANTABRIGIAE OMNIBUS AD QUOS HAE LIT-
TERAE PERVENERINT
SALUTEM
J. AVERY IX
PRO MERITIS EIUS AD GRADUM LITTERARUM DOC-
TORIS IN CULTORE
SUIS ADMISIMUS EIQUE DEDIMUS ET CONCESSIMUS
INSIGNIA
ET JURA OMNIA AD HUNC GRADUM PERTINENTIA DIE XIV
MENSIS JUNI ANNO DOMINI
MDCCCVC

"Now, you will notice," Sir Percival said in his best courtroom manner, tapping the parchment with his forefinger while his audience listened raptly, "the word 'Curatores' — referring, as one can readily imagine, to a place of cures.

This is followed by the word 'Universitatis.' The reference is clearly to the University Hospital, and since the only University Hospital in this part of the country in those olden days was the same University Hospital that graces Bloomsbury in London, on Gower Street between Grafton Way and University Street, I believe we can be assured that is the place referred to."

He looked about the room, taking in each attentive and intent face; then, satisfied, he continued.

"So John Avery begins by saying, 'Praeses Et Curatores Universitatis,' or, 'All praise to the University Hospital.' One might think he was simply thanking them for having worked some miraculous cure on him, but as we soon discover, his praise for the hospital has nothing to do with his health. It is based upon the fact that through the offices of the University Hospital, or, rather, one of its members, he was able to find a place to bury his treasure. Actually," he added, looking down his patrician nose at Clarence with the faintest touch of disappointment, "I should have thought that much would have been evident to the poorest of scholars."

"Just get on with it," Clarence said shortly.

"Yes, of course. Well," Sir Percival said, "it seems the hospital was not his first choice. He first thought of burying it near the 'Cantabrigiae Omnibus' — actually, in those days it was a stagecoach and not the type of omnibus we are accustomed to today — which left on its run to Canterbury, as we all know, from Euston Square, a short block from the hospital. But the site was unsatisfactory; you will note where he complains, 'Litterae Pervenerint Salutem,' indicating that the litter there prevented them from saluting — that is, selecting with pleasure — this first site. You must remember," he added, "that they spoke rather formally in those days."

They all nodded in agreement. Sir Percival's finger moved on the scroll to another line.

"However . . . one of their members — 'Eique Dedimus,' or 'dead Ike' in the vernacular of the fraternity — then took them to a small concession in the neighborhood — 'Concessimus Insignia,' or a concession that sold shoulder patches, and trophies, probably laurel wreaths as well, in those days — but again John Avery was frustrated in his efforts to find a suitable location for the burial of his treasure. We see the words 'Et Jura Omnia Ad Hunc Gradum Pertinentia,' which means that be swears all day that the grade — the land, that is — pertained to, or was owned by someone named Ad Hunc, undoubtedly a formidable opponent to frighten John Avery!"

He paused to see how he was doing with his audience. They were watching him, open-mouthed. Patience and faith, Pugh told himself, and went on.

"But John Avery was not a man to give up easily. You will note he mentions this 'doctoris in Cultore' — a cultured doctor, and quite obviously on the hospital staff. Either through threats or with the promise of money, John Avery forced the good doctor to give him the use of his quarters, the admissions office of the hospital — note, if you will, the 'Suis Admisimus' — and there, of course, is where John Avery, at long last, buried his treasure."

He shook his head sadly as Harold expelled a taut sigh of suspense-held breath.

"And what did the good doctor get for his help? He and thirteen others, undoubtedly the pirates who buried the gold and most certainly including Dead Ike, were made to die." He pointed to the words 'die XIV' and sighed. "It was all too common a practice in those days among the pirate fraternity, where treasure was concerned."

"I know. I read that someplace, too," Clarence said quietly, almost afraid to break the spell. He had been enthralled by the masterful exposition. He pointed. "But what's that Mensis Juni Anno Domini?"

"Mensis, Juni, Anno, and — last but not least — Domini?" Pugh sadly shook his head. "They were undoubtedly Italian sailors John Avery had brought with him to help bury the treasure and who, poor souls, he had to kill with the others in order to preserve the dark secret of his — literally — bloody gold."

Clarence nodded, his eyes shining. It all made sense. Had he only studied Latin in high school — but it was too late to worry about things like that at this late date. He put the past aside and pointed again.

"What about those letters at the very end?"

Pugh looked. "Oh, you refer to the MDCCCVC? That," he said with a glint of triumph in his eye, "together with the cross on the back — which really was not needed" — he glanced at Carruthers a bit reprovingly — "gives us the final clue as to the exact location of the treasure."

Clarence frowned. "How?"

"We know," Pugh explained patiently, "that some medical man, undoubtedly under compulsion, gave John Avery the use of the admissions office of the University Hospital for the burial of the gold. He could only have done so had he been in charge of that office at the time; otherwise he would have been treading upon the prerogatives of others, a quite un-English thing to do; and besides, there would not have been the privacy needed for the burial of the gold. But — "

He raised a finger; Clarence and the others watched that finger as if it were the magic wand of Merlin, or the bell of an oboe being played before a straw basket in India.

"But," Pugh repeated for emphasis, "*when* did all this happen? The parchment, unfortunately, does not give any dates. But what it *does* do is give us a healthy clue as to the identity of the doctor. And with this, of course, and the

knowledge that he was in charge of the admissions office, we can easily determine who he was, and during which years he functioned. And with these facts
we can easily determine where the admissions office was located during his
tenure." He spread his hands. "Simple."

Clarence nodded in agreement, although he was not convinced. "Right.
But — I mean, those letters? Just a few letters? How do they do all that?"

Pugh looked at him with a touch of disappointment.

"I should have thought that was self-evident. The letters are MDCCCVC.
Obviously the MD refers to the cultured physician we have been discussing
for what seems to be the last few days; his initials can only have been C.C.C.;
and he was the proud recipient at some stage in his life, of the Victoria Cross."

"Yeah. Sure. I'm sorry." Clarence was ashamed of himself for not having seen something that obvious. "And what about that x on the back of
the scroll?"

"Yes. Well," Pugh said, "the proper word for that is redundant, I believe."

"Redundant?"

"Yes. The person who put it there did not need to. It did not help in the
translation. But never mind." He turned the map over and exposed the hairline cracks and the small letter x. "My first thought, before giving the message sufficient thought, was that this was a map of a town, or an area of a
town, but it is now plain it is merely a plan of the University Hospital as it
appeared in the days of John Avery. It also is," he added, with another
reproving glance at Carruthers, "quite useless today. However, fortunately
these universities and their hospitals, particularly in England, keep exceedingly accurate records of their history, so a short visit to the hospital library
and I am sure I can emerge with the exact location of Dr. C.C.C.'s admissions
office in those distant days."

He brought out his pocket watch and sighed.

"I'm afraid my bridge must suffer this afternoon. I had best get to the
hospital library as soon as possible and find the proper spot for us to begin
our excavation."

"Wait a second! Wait a second! I can ask questions at a library as well as
you can!" Clarence eyed Sir Percival with distrust. "How do we know you
won't dig up the treasure and disappear?"

"I?" Sir Percival's eyebrows rose dramatically. "I, Sir Percival Pugh?
Disappear?" He made it sound on the order of the pyramids of Cheops disap-
pearing, or the Pacific Ocean. He smiled. "My dear sir, Pughs never disappear;
we seldom even fade, even temporarily. I am, frankly, far too well known to
disappear. And also, possibly more important from your standpoint, is the
packet I saw you place in the safe. If you know anything about me at all, you
should know there is no manner in which I would abandon twenty thousand

pounds, regardless of other riches to be won at the University Hospital, or anywhere else."

"Yeah, that's true — "

"However," Pugh said blithely, glancing at the safe in the corner with what seemed to be secret amusement, "if you wish to leave and leave us here — with Harold, of course — to guard the safe until your return, please feel free to do so."

"Hold it! Hold it!" Clarence had often suspected that Harold was privy to the safe's contents; after all, in Harold's days in Chicago he had been known as the king of the keisters, with a reputation for tearing safes apart with his bare hands if no other means appeared feasible, although with his skill that contingency seldom arose. And there was something in Pugh's secret smile that led Clarence to believe the safe and its contents had constituted a major portion of the conversational interchange between Sir Percival and Harold on the trip from Pugh's home to the farmhouse.

"Yes?" Pugh asked politely.

"Okay, you go — " That still didn't seem right. "Wait! We'll both go!" But that would leave Harold here with the safe and those three old buzzards, one of whom Harold was beginning to treat like his long-lost grandfather, and none of whom could be trusted any further than he could lift the Empire State Building. With one hand and a hernia. "Wait a second! I know — Harold will go with you." But how wise was that? If Harold couldn't keep his mouth shut — and he couldn't — and if he knew the combination to the safe — which seemed to be more and more a distinct possibility — and if Pugh got it out of him — which for a trial lawyer like Pugh had to be no great chore . . . . "No," Clarence said at last, beaten. "You go alone. "But," he added threateningly, "as you said yourself, you can't exactly disappear, a man in your position! And I can look a long, long time! Plus your three old pals stay here, and if you don't come back, and before dark, then — " He drew an illustrative finger across his throat.

Pugh looked at him with a slight frown of puzzlement.

"I cannot imagine why you could think I would not come back. I shall be here with the information in two shakes of a politician's hand." He moved toward the door. "And now, if you'll allow Harold to drive me to the station as being the most efficacious means of transport between this dismal swamp and London, I shall take the train and drive back in my own car. Which, I might mention, is a trifle more in keeping with my position than that miniature people-processor you have out there . . . . "

"Dr. Charles C. Coopersmith, V.C. MD, C.C.C., V.C., as advertised," Pugh announced modestly. He had deigned to accept a brandy from Harold, who was pouring with a look of profound admiration creasing his battered face. Pugh sipped and put aside his glass, bringing forth a bit of paper. "Here is a sketch I made. Dr. Coopersmith had his office, according to the old records in the hospital library, on the ground floor, obviously, since one could scarcely bury treasure by digging through an upper story. Today that area is just outside of a new building being used as a powerhouse. You will note the small x I have placed on the sketch, indicating a spot exactly three yards north and four yards east of the indicated corner of the building. It is here you must dig. It should give little trouble; the area is unpaved."

Clarence took the paper and studied it. "Grafton Way? Where's that? How do we get there?"

"I shall take my friends in my more commodious vehicle and you can follow with Harold in your car. I shall deliver you. When you find the treasure it may be too large for the trunk of your car, in which case we can relieve you of some of the weight."

"Oh, yeah? We'll manage," Clarence said and suddenly thought of something else, as he studied the sketch. "Hey! This x shows a spot outside of the building!"

"I said it was outside," Pugh said patiently. "One would scarcely expect the inside of a powerhouse to be unpaved."

"Yeah, but how are we going to dig outside of a building, in the open, without a lot of questions being asked? I figured in a powerhouse, with nobody around, or even just one guy Harold could handle, there'd be no problem. But outside — ?"

"Worry not," Pugh assured him with a wave of one manicured hand. "Should anyone ask you any questions, merely state that you are from the Gas Board, or the Electricity Board, if you prefer."

"But-at *night*?"

"People in major cities would be highly suspicious if you dug at any other time," Pugh said positively. Clarence, thinking about it, knew he was right. Pugh glanced at his watch. "We'd best be going."

"Right," Clarence said. He took another look at the sketch, admiring its detail. The entire affair was quite exciting to him; with the sketch in his hand it seemed to move from the dreamlike fantasy he had felt while the parchment was being deciphered, to the hard reality of the possibility of hard cash. Twenty million bucks! He shook his head and then thought of something. "Me and Harold," he announced. "We'll do the hard work, the digging. The old men are too old, and you — you don't have the proper clothes for the job."

"True," Sir Percival said, admitting the undeniable fact. "We shall, instead, stand by and cheer on your efforts. Pretend you are Eton and Harold is

Harrow. Make a sporting event out of it, so to speak. Possibly even lay a bob or two on who strikes oil — or gold — first — "

"You don't have to do that," Clarence said hastily. "No sense in bringing a crowd to watch us. While we're digging, you go to a pub and enjoy yourself."

"You're sure our huzzas would not stimulate you in your efforts?"

"Positive. You go get yourself a beer."

"If you insist," Pugh said graciously, "but while we are gone, our thoughts shall ever be with you. Dig, we shall be saying silently, wherever we are; dig and may you enjoy your toil."

"'Good friend, for Jesu's sake forbear,'" Simpson quoted, "'to dig the dust enclosed here.' Shakespeare's epitaph," he explained, rather pleased with himself, and then seemed to realize what he had said. "Well, I don't really mean you should forbear, of course," he added hastily. "Shakespeare isn't buried anywhere near the University Hospital."

"'Dig till you gently perspire,'" Briggs donated. "That's Kipling." Kipling had always been more Briggs's cup of tea than Shakespeare. "Only dig!"

"'Dig we must,'" Harold suddenly said. He had been silent most of the day and the strain was telling. "That's Con Ed in New York," he added proudly.

"Yes," Pugh said, before Carruthers might be tempted to contribute. He glanced at his watch. "But however you do it, you'd best get on with it, or you'll still be digging after dawn in daylight, and that would, indeed, appear conspicuous."

"Right!" Clarence said, champing at the bit. "Hal, get that pick and shovel from the barn, and the lantern there, too. And then let's go!" He picked up the scroll, rolled it into a tube and tucked it into his pocket, turning to Pugh. "You lead the way!"

"A pleasure," Pugh said, and led the way.

They came down the Western Avenue Extension in tandem, looking somewhat as if Pugh's limousine might be towing Clarence's smaller car, came through Lisson Grove to the Marylebone Road, past Regents Park station into Gower Street. Pugh slowed down, turning once again into Grafton Way and drew to the curb. Behind him Clarence also came to a stop; a moment later he was out of the car and inspecting the area. He nodded and bent through the window of the limousine.

"That's the powerhouse?"

"Exactly."

"Good. I'll take it from here," Clarence said in a low voice. "And thanks. Now you four go off and get yourself a beer or two at some pub, and we'll get together later. If we don't see you here, we'll see you back at the house." He smiled. "Have a good time."

116

"We shall do our best," Pugh said bravely, and waved a hand. A moment later he had driven off.

Behind him Clarence suddenly frowned as he watched the tail lights of the limousine turn into Tottenham Court Road and disappear. He had expected far more opposition from Pugh, or at least from Carruthers — and definitely from the runt, Briggs — to his being left alone with Harold at the site of the treasure, and he had prepared many fine arguments to get them to leave. It was odd that they left so easily; suspicious, really. It was certain that under no circumstance would he have been talked out of standing right there and watching every move of the opposition had the shoe been on the other foot.

Then he smiled. Pugh, undoubtedly, was on his way back to the farmhouse at top speed, ready to tackle the safe while they worked at the treasure. Well, if that was the case, more power to him. True, there was fifty grand of Clarence's money in that safe, along with forty each from Pugh and the old men, but that was a drop in the bucket compared to the treasure he was digging for. And if Pugh thought he, Clarence, was going to return to the farmhouse just for that measly sixty grand, if he found the treasure, then Sir Percival was dreaming.

And even if they didn't find the treasure, Pugh still wouldn't have that safe open before they got back; it was a lot tougher safe than maybe it appeared. And if he found that Pugh had been monkeying with the safe when he got back — if he found it necessary to go back — then Pugh and the old men were going to lose their share of the dough in the safe! But one thing was sure; Pugh couldn't bust into the safe, so let them try until hell froze over, or the brandy and champagne ran out at the house, whichever came first.

With a grin he jerked his head at Harold and walked over to mark the spot to start their excavation.

15

There was a time, in the memory of ancients, when a hospital worried more about the curing of patients and less about the physical conditions under which these cures were effected. One wonders how Florence Nightingale, going her nightly rounds, made do with a mere candle, rather than the multitudinous collection of rheostat-modulated, varying-wattage, multiple-voltage, floor, desk, wall, ceiling, or handheld lamps. One ponders her remarkable ability to dispense needed nostrums under conditions of sweltering heat, rather than find indispensable properly installed, direction-oriented, humidity-controlled, temperature-regulated air-conditioning units. One is dumbfounded by her ability to entertain a patient with a smile and a small squeeze of the hand, rather than requiring the presence of a battery of good-will ladies, a traveling library, AM-FM stereo radios, or one of those full-color, remote-controlled, gooseneck-mounted television receivers that make up in drugging the patient what the pharmacist has failed to provide.

Clarence Wellington Alexander, however, would have been the last to cavil at the modern improvements in hospital equipment; because of them, there also were required huge powerhouses, and it was within the protective shade of one that he and Harold now stood. The building was windowless, and of a size that would have given pause to the pyramid builders, forced the erectors of Machu Picchu to second thoughts, and even led the Easter Islanders to seriously consider miniatures. It loomed over the two men like the Great Wall of China, and gave them complete protection from the stares of possible passers-by. It was pleasant to think that London was still a city where one could peacefully excavate a treasure in the middle of the night without every householder in the neighborhood poking his nose in your business. New York, Clarence knew, would never meet these high standards.

He checked the sketch by the light of a street lamp, and then proceeded to march to the proper corner of the huge building. Here he took a deep breath and marched off the proper number of paces north and then the proper number east that the sketch called for, pleased that he was walking on grass, which should be simple to dig through. At the proper point he started to dig in his heel to mark the spot where Harold could begin to wield the pick and shovel, but to his surprise, at that particular point it seemed the grass had been replaced by a heavy steel plate of some sort. With a frown Clarence lit the lantern and stared down. Facing him in the ground was this steel plate, apparently firmly fixed and obviously marking something. He bent closer; written across its face was the word: DANGER.

Clarence's frown deepened. In the light of the lantern he checked the sketch again, but there was no doubt he was at the correct spot, give or take a few inches. He looked at the steel plate again, noting small letters above and below the larger word DANGER. He got to his knees, holding the lantern at a favorable angle to read the message. It was all too clear. Above the DAN-GER it read: *Do Not Excavate in This Area*, while below it simply said: *High Tension Electricals Below*. As if to emphasize the importance of the warning, some electrician at some time had added in white paint the numbers, *50,000 volts*.

Clarence knew exactly what fifty thousand volts could do to a person; he had seen too many James Cagney prison movies not to know. A horrible suspicion began to form in his brain. He came to his feet, brushing the knees of his trousers automatically, and then walked back to the car, turning the lantern off as he walked. Harold, puzzled by this inexplicable change in plans, followed along obediently, carrying the pick and shovel. At the car Clarence set down the lantern and turned to his large companion. His face was white, his eyes glazed. He seemed to speak with an effort.

"Shove everything in the trunk and wait for me," he said with a deadly quiet to his voice. This was a Clarence that Harold had never known, a Clarence that Harold suspected could be dangerous. "I'll be back in a couple of minutes."

He turned and walked off without waiting for an answer. A strange buzzing sound began to form in his head, a buzzing he had not heard for years, and he knew it heralded a complete and violent loss of temper. But he also knew he had to control it, at least for the moment. He mounted the steps of the hospital as in a dream, and found himself facing an information desk with an uniformed nurse behind it. His questions and her answers seemed to him to come from two different people standing off to one side, hidden in the gloom of the vaulted entrance, speaking through echo-chambers. He saw her shake her head and had to concentrate on what she was saying, for it seemed to him that her head was still and that it was the building that had moved. It was very disconcerting. He concentrated harder.

No, the hospital had no library for records or for anything else. The university across the way had a library, of course, except it obviously would not be open at this hour. Latin? A bit, she said in a puzzled tone; why? To interpret something? If she could. Oh, this — yes, as the gentleman suspected, it was a diploma, a Cambridge diploma for something in the animal-husbandry field, or the agricultural field, she thought; she wasn't quite certain of all the words, but in general there seemed to be little doubt that —

But she was speaking to empty space. Clarence had left and was walking a bit unsteadily down the steps of the hospital. The man, the nurse thought professionally, looked as if he could use some of the care the hospital dispensed, but soliciting custom was against the hospital rules . . . .

Sir Percival, Carruthers, Simpson, and Briggs had, indeed, taken Clarence's advice, and were sitting in one corner of a smoke-filled pub, enjoying — yes, actually enjoying — mugs of ale, now that Sir Percival had offered to pay for brandy and champagne. Sir Percival, while a lover of money, was none the less a most generous host; still, they did not feel it right to take advantage of him. Besides, in their unspoken thoughts, was the idea that they had better get used to ale or beer again; in fact, they knew they would be lucky to have this simple fare to fall back upon in the future.

"Ale," Carruthers said, and considered his mug. "It's all a matter of mental conditioning, I suppose. Liking it, I mean," he added, and downed the contents of his mug with gusto. He tapped on the table to indicate to the serving wench his need for a refill, waited for it, and dipped his nose into it with fervor.

"I agree," Simpson said, puffing on a tarlike bit of rope that passed for a cigar, and trying his best to savor it. "It's all in looking at it in the proper manner. I recall a situation one of my characters got himself into — Limehouse Louie, I believe it was. Anyway, it seems he drew this ten-year sentence, and he knew that since he suffered from claustrophobia, if he didn't condition himself to liking it, he was going to suffer. And when the ten years were up — "

"He asked to stay!" Briggs said sarcastically.

Simpson beamed at him. "You read the book!"

"What I am curious about," Carruthers said idly, "is how far Harold and Clarence will dig before they come to the proper conclusion that they have been had."

"Not very far," Pugh predicted, and smiled. "Or at least I hope so for Harold's sake, since I imagine he'll be doing any work that is done. You see, I am a trustee of the hospital, and I was present at the inauguration of that powerhouse. Many cables and things . . . . ."

He did not explain nor did they ask him to. They were all relaxed, feeling the effects of several ales with little food in their stomachs. Briggs burped gently and frowned.

"What *I* am curious about," he said, "is what Clarence's reaction is going to be when he discovers it was all a put-on." He looked at Pugh. "When you go back to the farm, he's apt to be — well, irritated, to say the least."

Pugh looked at him with faint amusement.

"And why on earth would you think I might go back to that squalid place?" Briggs stared, confused.

"Well," he said, "what about your twenty thousand quid? Our stock certificates are worthless, but I saw that money of yours with my own eyes. That was real lolly. That wasn't counterfeit!"

"Heavens, no!" Pugh said, and raised his eyes ceiling-ward. "From Barclay's? And at any rate, how could I possibly have foisted counterfeit on Clarence with him standing at my elbow when I collected it? Counting it over my shoulder as the teller shoved the stuff at me?"

"Well, then — ?" Simpson asked, a puzzled expression on his horselike face.

Pugh looked from one frowning face to another and then sighed.

"If you will finish your drinks and come to my home-where I sincerely hope you will accept brandy and champagne, since we have neither beer nor ale — I shall be pleased to explain." He raised his hand for the bill, paid it after close examination, and came to his feet. "Gentlemen — ?"

Pugh paused in the foyer to glance through the evening Journal, and then followed his guests into the living room, carrying his briefcase, which he had brought from his car. He rang for the butler, gave the appropriate orders, and waited until they were carried out. Then, comfortably seated with the others, he raised his glass in a toast.

"Cheers."

"Cheers." It was a chorused echo.

They all sipped, after which Sir Percival patted his lips, put away his handkerchief, and looked from one to the other of the three men facing him. He shook his head as if with disappointment.

121

"To be frank," he said, "my feelings are hurt to have persons who I should have imagined would have respect for me, think for one moment that I would give a twister such as Clarence the correct hour, let alone twenty thousand of the best, even temporarily." He reached over, bringing his bag to him and opening it, bringing out a package wrapped in brown paper. He opened it and inspected the contents before looking up. "Now, these stock certificates, I believe, are yours." He handed them over to a stunned Carruthers. "This twenty thousand pounds in new notes, of course, is mine." He placed the bundle to one side. "And the remaining forty thousand dollars that Clarence was kind enough to donate to the common cause, I suggest we divide equally, since we contributed equally to its acquisition."

The three were staring at the money speechlessly. Pugh sighed.

"My dear chaps — you had the audacity to murder ten people, nine of them with impunity. On the S.S. *Sunderland* you managed to cheat at shipboard horse racing, the first time it has ever been attempted, let alone successfully, to my knowledge. You invented the game of Burmese Solitaire and used it not only to take several thousand pounds from some card cheats, but also to get me to defend you without a fee — an even rarer situation, believe me! In your day you wrote some of the most imaginative mystery novels around. Now, Carruthers conceives of this pirate-treasure ploy. Yet you do not recognize a simple switch of brown paper packages when you see it." Pugh frowned. "Carruthers, as I said, you conceived of that pirate-treasure business. Tell me, why did you do it if not for some gain?"

Carruthers looked abashed.

"I had hoped," he said rather shamefacedly, "that when Clarence and Harold went off to dig for pirate treasure someplace, we might — well, break into the cupboard and make off with a few bottles of . . . . " He allowed the words to trail into silence, and then added apologetically, "We're getting old, you know . . . . "

"I see. Well, in that case, possibly we should divide that forty thousand dollars in a different manner," Pugh said thoughtfully, but there was a twinkle in his eye. "One portion sufficient for your needs as far as brandy and champagne are concerned — let us say an amount equivalent to what the cupboard may have held — I leave it to your honesty to make the estimate — and the balance to me."

"Hey! Here! None of that!" Briggs said, outraged, and turned to the others. "Look at him, would you! What did I tell you about him? Twenty thousand dollars he gets for a few hours' work, work on a scheme Billy-Boy thought up, and he's still not satisfied! He — !"

"Tim!" Carruthers said sternly. "Be quiet!"

"I will not be quiet! I — "

He paused, as he seemed to have lost his audience. They had all turned at a discreet cough from the butler, heard above Briggs's diatribe through long practice on the butler's part. Pugh nodded.

"Yes, Symes?"

"That — that — that gentleman who was here just this morning, Sir Percival," Symes began, but before he could go further, Harold pushed into the room. He was alone and seemed in some sort of a daze.

"Yes?" Pugh asked politely.

Harold looked around the room slowly. His eyes seemed to focus only when they came to Carruthers.

"Pops — "

"Yes, Harold?" Carruthers said in a kindly tone.

"Pops, I didn't know where else to look for you. I — " He stopped.

"What's the trouble, Harold?" Carruthers' tone was soothing.

Harold swallowed and took a deep breath, as if to furnish power for a speech he hated to make but knew he had to.

"Pops — when we got back to the farmhouse, Clare, he run right into the house, so I come in after him and he's at the safe. And when he got it open and saw the package only had newspaper inside, he said — " Harold paused.

"What did Clarence say, Harold?"

"He was like a maniac, pops. A real maniac. I seen a guy like that went off his nut in Joliet, once, tried to bite right through the cell bars. Bust all his teeth before they drag him loose . . . . "

"What did Clarence say, Harold?"

"He — he said he was goin' to kill all you guys. He meant it. I know, I seen guys like that before. They don't care what happens to them, they're so mad. And he said if I didn't go along and help, he'd start the killing with me. He meant it, pops. He had a gun in the safe along with the rest of the dough, had it in a little box I never knew what was in it before —"

For the first time Pugh interrupted.

"How much money was there, Harold?"

"Nine grand, six hundred. I counted it afterward — "

Carruthers cast a reproachful look at Pugh and then went back to Harold. "After what, Harold?"

"After I hit him with the shovel," Harold said simply, and suddenly sat down in a chair, staring at his hands.

The police, called at Pugh's insistence as an officer of the court, had taken away a still dazed, unresisting Harold. The others in the room, feeling somewhat in shock, stared at each other silently. At last Simpson spoke, a look of sadness on his long, thin face; he spoke for them all.

123

"Poor Harold . . . . "

"But, certainly," Carruthers said, looking at Pugh, "it's a simple case of self-defense?"

Pugh shook his head.

"It would be a most difficult defense, and one I should never think any advocate worth his salt would even faintly consider. Look at the evidence: an open safe, nine thousand six hundred dollars in American money to be quarreled over; a record — which I am sure their housekeeper will testify to when she is located — that Clarence's treatment of Harold was always of contempt; Harold's record of violence in the United States, while Clarence's record is one of nonviolence. Add to that the fact that the police would have only Harold's unsupported word that Clarence had gone mad with anger and was capable of, and planning, our murders. Then, when you add to all that the size of Harold, as opposed to the size of Clarence, and I'm afraid that self-defense would be a most difficult case to support."

It was all too true, and they all knew it.

"It looks hopeless," Briggs said glumly.

Pugh looked at him in total surprise.

"Do you think so? I shouldn't think so at all. Quite the contrary, as a matter of fact."

They all looked at him. "But you said — " Simpson began.

"I said self-defense was a poor defense. That's all I said." Pugh glanced at the wall clock. "And now I'm afraid it's getting a bit late, and I shall have to be up in the morning to have a word with Harold in prison and get him to recall a bit more accurately the events of the evening."

"Can we possibly contribute a bit of money toward Harold's defense?" Carruthers asked anxiously. "Out of our share of that forty thousand dollars?"

"Wait a second — !" Briggs began hotly.

"It will not be necessary," Pugh said before Briggs could continue. "I shall be content to take this case just for the nine thousand six hundred dollars that Harold possesses." He walked them to the door and paused in the foyer. "If you wish, though," he added, "you might consider paying Harold's air fare back to the United States. He will be quite destitute after paying my fee."

Briggs opened his mouth to scream, but again Pugh spoke before the little man could get a sound out.

"You really can well afford it," Sir Percival said gently. "I see in tonight's papers that the Namibian Chartered Mines did not go dry, after all; it seems it was merely a false rumor begun by one of the company directors in a vain attempt to corner all the shares at a vastly reduced price. He is being held by the authorities at the moment, and the stock, since his arrest, has gone up almost double in price to what it was a week ago . . . . "

16

S ir Percival Pugh stood and considered the jury a moment. They looked like almost all the juries he had ever faced, eagerly awaiting his expertise to clarify the confusion created by the prosecution for the Crown, Sir Osbert Willoughby, in his opening remarks. At last, satisfied, Sir Percival nodded and turned first to the judge, and then back to the jury.

"My Lord, gentlemen of the jury. I have heard my worthy opponent claim that my client, Harold Nishbagel, did willfully and with malice aforethought — those words not being original with my worthy opponent, I might mention, despite his attempt to make them appear so — take a shovel and beat his long-time friend and close associate, Clarence Wellington Alexander, to death.

"Gentlemen, my Lord, nothing could be further from the truth. Harold Nishbagel would not harm a fly. I have three witnesses to this fact, witnesses of such unimpeachable probity that even Sir Osbert will be forced to accept their irrefutable honesty. They will testify to Harold Nishbagel's unflagging kindness and dislike of anything smacking of violence. I might mention in passing, gentlemen, that Nishbagel, in its original Osage Indian language, means exactly that — kind-heartedness, moderation, abatement, tranquillity.

To an Osage named Nishbagel, doing anything of a forceful nature would be to violate the code of the Osages, and bring upon one the curse of all his Osage ancestors."

Sir Percival paused to sip a glass of water. He dabbed at his lips while watching the jury from the corner of his eye. Their own eyes, like those of a sparrow locked in frozen rigidity to those of a snake, followed his every move. Gotcha! Pugh thought with uncharacteristic reversion to his Irish ancestors, and went on, his voice calmly continuing to hypnotize them.

"Gentlemen, what are the true facts of this case? Did Harold Nishbagel raise a shovel and bring it down upon the head of his friend, Clarence Wellington Alexander? Yes, gentlemen, he did."

(Sensation)

"Yes, gentlemen, he did. That is a fact, and facts are not to be denied. They are, however, to be extrapolated, to be explained. I stated earlier, gentlemen, that Harold Nishbagel would not harm a fly, and that is true. But a wasp? Gentlemen, in the Osage Nation, the wasp is the deadliest of enemies, representing as it does all the evils in mankind. It also stings, gentlemen, as many of us know to our sorrow; it also stings. Only those who have suffered the sting of that member of the family hymenoptera can know how painful it can be. And so, gentlemen, when my client saw this wasp on the forehead of his beloved friend, he raised his hand to strike it. In his anxiety to relieve his friend of the possibility of that painful bite, he failed to realize that at the moment he was holding a shovel . . . . "

Pugh paused and then gave the prosecution its death blow.

"My worthy opponent had made much of the fact that there was no sign of any wasp in the wound; and that, gentlemen, is the true tragedy of this case, and one that requires that you not only find my client innocent, but that you add your commiseration to mine. For not only did my client forget he was holding a shovel, he also missed the stinging beast, killing his best friend. That, gentlemen, is tragedy . . . . "

He sighed.

"Gentlemen, my first witness is William Carruthers . . . . "

The northeast corner of the lounge of the Mystery Authors Club was ringing with cheer. Two extra chairs had been brought there, and while it made for a slight bit of crowding, it did nothing to lessen the festivities that emanated from the alcove.

"Five of them, now!" Potter, the secretary, said to one of his coterie, looking darkly toward the source of all the merriment.

"One of them is Sir Percival Pugh!" someone said in awe.

"And the big one is the man he just defended, that Indian," someone else said. "But he'll be leaving soon. I saw him leave his bags with the hall porter, and the hall porter told me the man wanted to be called in an hour to catch the airport bus."

"Good riddance," Potter said, and sniffed. "Any idiot too stupid to notice he was holding a shovel when he went to swat a wasp! And then to *miss* the beast, yet! Can't be very bright, is all I can say."

"Oh, I don't know," someone else said. "He had the brains to hire Sir Percival, didn't he?"

"And it wasn't his intelligence that was at fault," someone else said, "just his aim. Happens to the best of us. I remember at the last August skeet shoot — "

Potter walked away. He hated to be disagreed with, especially by members of his own clique. He glared toward the northeast corner. Maybe if he started with just the three old men, and then had them *really* disappear one at a time . . . . But he had a feeling that with his ill fortune, the three would be around for a long, long time . . . or that someone else had used the plot a long time before . . . .

About the Author

ROBERT L. FISH, the youngest of three children, was born on August 21,1912 in Cleveland, Ohio. He attended the local schools in Cleveland and went to Case University (now Case-Western Reserve) where he graduated with a degree in Mechanical Engineering. He married Mamie Kates, also from Cleveland, and they had two daughters. Mr. Fish worked as a civil engineer, traveling and moving throughout the United States. In 1953 he was asked to set up a plastics factory in Rio de Janeiro, Brazil. He and his family moved to Brazil where they remained for nine years. He played golf and bridge in the little spare time he had. One rainy weekend in the late 1950's, when the weather prohibited Mr. Fish from playing golf, he sat down and wrote a short story that he submitted to Ellery Queen Mystery Magazine. When that story was accepted, Mr. Fish continued to write short stories. In 1962 Mr. Fish returned to the United States; he took one year to write full-time and then he returned to engineering and writing. His first novel, THE FUGITIVE, won him an Edgar Award for the Best First Mystery. When his health prevented him from working on both careers, he retired from engineering and spent his time writing. His published works include over forty books and countless short stories. "Mute Witness" was made into a movie starring Steve McQueen. Mr. Fish died February 23,1981 at his home in Connecticut. Each year at the annual Mystery Writers of America dinner, a memorial award is presented in his name for the best first short story; this is fitting, as Mr. Fish was always eager to assist young writers in their field.

Printed in the United Kingdom by
Lightning Source UK Ltd., Milton Keynes
141495UK00001B/58/A